Seafood Porridge

Nicholas Kyte

Seafood Porridge

By Nicholas Kyte

Dedication

This book is dedicated to all the hard-working teachers and educators who strive to give their students a great future.

My thanks to Jackie, family and friends for their support in writing the story.

Seafood Porridge

MICHAELMAS TERM

SEPTEMBER

*"Care about what other people think and you will always be
their prisoner"*

*Lao Tsu
(604 BC – 531 BC)*

Chapter 1

The Chairman of the Board of Governors and the Headmaster invite all members of staff and their spouses / partners to the New Academic Year Dinner, in the Main House at 1900 hours on 2 September. Dress: Formal. RSVP

THE email signalled the start of yet another school year and created an opportunity for teachers who had not seen one another over the long summer recess to catch up with each other's adventures or otherwise. Over the forthcoming days there would follow the familiarisation and induction for new teachers, riveting inset training, and a bit of departmental time.

The staff had started to refer to the principal Deputy Head as the HMD - Head Master Designate. It rolled off the tongue easily, and somehow had a good commercial ring to it, corporate even, right up there with CEO, President and Chairman. The other Deputy Heads were quite simply Deputies to the Sheriff waiting to get his star.

"I know this invitation is from the Headmaster," said Julie from the Maths Department. "But what is actually going on? The old one is still in office on paper but will actually be away inducting into his new appointment, and the new one has been appointed but cannot take up the position for a term because the other hasn't moved out."

"Probably best you don't ask," her companion replied.

"He's probably getting two salaries, one from here and one from the new place. You can see who's on the top table. Anyway, I am looking forward to the meal – it was absolutely incredible last year: the cook is an ex-army chef who knows what he is doing."

So the dinner jackets, bow ties and smart dinner dresses waited patiently out on the patio, holding in one hand the red or white wine that they had been served, clutching in the other the plate of hors d'oeuvres that needed a third hand to actually eat from.

Finally it was time to go in, and those wise ones who had looked at the seating plan previously proceeded like Speedy Boarders, whilst the rest queued and having reached the table plan fathomed out where to go. But as is so often the case, the seating plan on the wall was not orientated to match the tables on the ground, and consequently each guest spent more time than necessary as they mentally turned the piece of paper round to make sense of where to go, less easy after a glass of wine than before.

It was convivial, with bemused new teachers and still more bemused partners entertained by already established staff; and fellow colleagues-in-arms reminisced over those who had left, enviously perhaps, and turned their attentions slowly and reluctantly to the future. For some there was a "Here we go again" feeling, whilst for others the routine offered a protection from the rigours of life and its realities beyond the cosiness of academia. For all, however, the meal was a meeting point and, more importantly still, it was free.

The meals were served by kitchen staff nobly assisted by some Sixth form girls who had been co-opted for the evening. The soup was followed by salmon parcels with white sauce and green beans; dessert was a piece of cheddar with grapes. Wine on the table was slightly better than plonk, and on the basis of one bottle per four people. It was necessary to have been kind to the kitchen staff to improve on the quantity, but there was no way to improve on the quality other than to have brought it in personally.

"I don't think the menu is as good as last year," a voice muttered. "We had a far better choice last time, and there was a big Stilton as well. I realise that this is a freebie, but actually the wine is a bit ordinary as well!"

"Uhm," added another. "And I have been watching what the top table is being served as well. They are not having the same as us, I've noticed – the Chairman, Head and Deputy Heads are getting totally different food. Doesn't look like the wine on their table has got the same label on the bottles as ours either. Upstairs and Downstairs".

The ringing out from the top table of a superior bottle struck with a superior knife filled the room and the diners hushed. The Chairman of the Board of Governors stood up, a humourless man who earned his living in a very dignified firm of accountants.

"Headmaster, Deputy Headmasters, members of staff old and new, and spouses: Good evening to you."

It was all too easy to sit back with the satisfaction of a filled belly, and the wine doing gentle circuits around the head, and basically not really listen to the old fellow. But professional etiquette prevailed. He commented on the poor state of the economy, and the fact that an independent school somewhere in the country had had to shut over the holidays. And it was then that everyone developed a touch of indigestion.

"You are all very lucky to have a job at all in the current climate. We are working hard not to make any redundancies and to that end the Board of Governors has taken the decision to freeze salary levels for this year. Staff at an independent school not so far from here have lost their jobs as a result of the closure, and I say again that you are lucky to have your jobs and you should count your blessings."

He finally sat down to a less than enthusiastic round of applause. A voice on a table at the furthest from the top table was heard to observe sardonically:

"Great start – hope they don't choke on the port I see they are having. One, two, three, four ...."

"What are you doing?"

"I'm counting my blessings".

"Let it go, Mike. We've had a half decent meal with good people around us. Could be worse, could have been sitting on the top table with the Senior Management Team, and the Chairman. It's a shame the Head is leaving – for all his shortcomings he leaves us alone to get on with the job."

"Yes, I agree" said another. "Anyway it matters little

what the Chairman might think of us: with *us* he is staffed, without us he is stuffed. Without *him*, would we notice the difference?"

It was as the guests started to leave the dining room that one of the ladies squealed as she went up the steps out of the dining room. A fast moving furry shape scrabbled up the steps in front of her, and disappeared into the hallway.

"It was a rat," she said, with a tremor in her voice. "A goddam rat for heaven's sake."

And the guests sobered slightly and made their way under the moonlit sky back to their cars to go home.

Chapter 2

THE day after the dinner was Sunday, and served as a lull before the impending storm as the first week of term unfolded. But by seven in the evening the email dropped into the electronic mailbox that was to be the pattern of events every Sunday thereafter:

All staff are reminded that there is a full day of meetings starting at 8.30 am promptly. All are expected to attend.

0830 Coffee
0900 Headmaster's address
1000 Safeguarding
1045 Coffee
1115 First Aid re-qualification
1300 Lunch
1400 Heads of Department
1500 Departmental time

Staff cars started to fill the car park soon after eight on Monday and the occupants made their way to the staffroom for the first caffeine fix of the day. The atmosphere was both cautious and exuberant, the holidays had finished but lessons had not yet started. Boxes of text books were accumulating in the corridors, and would need to be checked against the lists of books that had been ordered months ago.

Stationery items for the first term were begging to be put in the stationery stores, but would have to wait a while.

The out-going Headmaster stood at the front of the hall and waited for the last of the staff to take their seats, clutching their cups of coffee, trying not to spill it.

"Good, er, Good Morning everyone. I want to keep this part as short as I can because er, because there is a lot to get through this morning. A warm welcome to the new members of staff - I, er I won't ask you to stand up and introduce yourselves. Always seems a bit of an embarrassment."

He turned his attention to the large screen and started to go over the statistical analysis of the public exam results, by which the school was solely measured. Lots of charts and projections and fundamental black magic that could not alter the outcome already achieved, merely inform for the next meeting in a year's time.

"As you know, I am leaving at the end of term, though, er, I shall not be here much during the term, as I, er, work my way into my new job. I retain executive control, whilst day-to-day responsibilities fall to the Senior Deputy Head. For the benefit of the new staff, following a rigorous and transparent round of interviews, er, the Senior Deputy Head will be taking over from me as Headmaster as at Christmas, and he is in the meantime the Headmaster Designate. Thank you for your time."

Safeguarding came next, and underpinned everything that took place. No-one in the school wanted the children not to feel safe and comfortable in their environment. Well, nearly everyone, since the hidden and secret agendas of some brought anything other than security and safeguarding to the table. But some of the safeguarding was protecting children from parental abuse and from self-abuse. It might have made sense to have Teacher safeguarding in addition to Children safeguarding since the staff were the filling in the sandwich of naughty children and protective parents on one side, and very often autocratic and self-protective Senior Management on the other.

"Is it really three years since we last did the First Aid? Oh well, here we go: what group am I in?"

Julie from Maths headed off to the lists, ascertained who she should be with and set to practising CPR. This seemed to comprise quite a lot of chatting about life in general, since only one person at a time could try to revive the manikin with CPR. Nonetheless, it was good to have skills in hand for eventualities one might hope never to have to face.

Patsy Brown from the History Department really could not see why she should be doing it. She always had a lot to say about everything, mostly critical, and always lengthy. She was considerably past her sell-by date but did not dare retire for financial reasons: not much planning and too much partying in the past were coming home to roost. In all likelihood she was not wrong - any attempt on her part to administer CPR might have resulted in a further casualty.

As the staff members were preparing to leave the hall, they were directed to the printed timetables that were being issued to Heads of Department, and these in turn were handing them out to members of their respective departments. Thirsty bodies hauled themselves over to the coffee table. Thoughts moved ruggedly to the arrival of the students in two days' time, and words to the timetables they had just received, as they scanned the details.

"You know, we were promised the timetables by the end of last term, and only now do we get them – and mine's dreadful. I've looked at some of the classes, and I actually have to get from one end of the campus to the other and then back again from one class to the next. You know how awful the weather can be when winter sets in, so it's going to be a bundle of fun."

"I know. I was told that I would get the A block, promised it in fact, and here I am with B block on my timetable. I can't see why they need to keep changing the timetable every year anyway. Get one sorted that works, and stick to it."

And so it was that Wednesday finally arrived, and with it the coaches that brought the students in from miles around. As if by some long-established tradition, but in reality a new initiative, three deputy heads stood as a presence whilst the coaches disgorged their human cargo. Three deputy heads who were wearing suits that might accompany a hearse. Three deputy heads who did little to interact meaningfully with the tide of young humans that went past, preferring rather to josh around together engrossed in some private set of jokes and agendas. The supervision of the stream of students more or less well dressed in school uniform was delegated to an underling staff member who halted traffic or students accordingly as they tackled the pedestrian crossing.

The same process, but in reverse, would take place at half past five through to six o'clock when the youngsters headed off to the waiting coaches to get home after a long day's attendance.

A juxtaposition made itself apparent. There was the divide between upper echelons and lower echelons of staff; and there was the divide between adults and youngsters. This was an approximation of the situation, since there were those staff members of lower echelon who interacted on a far more familiar basis with the upper echelons; and there were those members of staff who interacted on a far friendlier basis with the students.

Chapter 3

THERE had arrived the previous day on a flight from Hong Kong a young lad joining for a year to improve his English. Menn's father was a retained Marine Biologist, now retired from full-time employment, who had held a government position in the Department for Agriculture, Fisheries and Conservation, tackling the not-infrequent problems faced by the fish farmers. Now Menn's older brother had followed suit and among other duties went out to fish farms collecting samples of fish stocks contaminated by Red Tides. Somehow Menn's father had secured funding for his son to go to England for a year to study, and an agency had got him placed in the school to learn English thoroughly before going on to university.

As Menn went through the entrance gates, he stared in surprise at the sight of the former stately home that had become the site of a private and independent school. It rose up magnificently at the end of a drive that in a previous incarnation had seen horses and carriages carrying ladies and gentlemen; and that now saw the daily arrival of coaches carrying students. The slightly austere building that would be home for the year seemed to reach out in welcome.

Menn was already eighteen, older than most

others in the Upper Sixth, but part of a group that was doing a third year in the Sixth Form as preparation for Oxford or Cambridge. Among other things, he had brought with him the clothes that he wore to do the Tai Chi and Shaolin Kung Fu that he had been studying for a decade and had no intention of abandoning during his stay in England. He had a room to himself in the Sixth Form block, and slipped into the routines of an English boarding school.

At the beginning of the third week of term, a parcel arrived from Hong Kong for Menn, and he took it up to his room to open it excitedly. He tore open the packaging and extracted from the box a Moon Cake. His mouth began to water at the thought of eating the delicacy, with its finely crafted symbol imprinted on the surface. He rushed off to find the Boarding House Master:

"Sir, Sir! I have a Moon Cake. In Hong Kong it is *Jung-chau Jit* on Monday, Moon Festival. Can I have permission to stay up for midnight to have lantern and eat Moon Cake?"

"I think it is a bit late, Menn. If we let you do it, we will have to let everyone do it."

"Oh, Sir, no fair – is Chinese tradition, always in my family we do this. Also is *deng mi*, lantern riddle"

"Sorry, Menn. It's the people at the top that don't

understand those sort of things and don't want them to happen – while you are with us at this school, you are going to have to make some sacrifices."

Somewhat crestfallen, Menn made his way back to his room, and gave thought to what the Housemaster had said. That evening he looked up at the sky and stared wistfully up at the moon that was days away from being full, and then looked at the Moon Cake his mother had sent him and thought hard. He looked at the piece of paper on which he had written his riddle to share with others if not with his family. He went to the Housemaster's office and after knocking politely poked his head inside. He was sitting at his desk, and looked up as Menn came in.

"Sir, I share with you *deng mi*, I share with you my riddle: *'Why you go green when you ill?'*"

"I don't know, Menn. You tell me."

"Sir, cannot tell you; you must guess. I come back another time."

With which Menn withdrew, smiling at his joke, and feeling happier with life. He went to his room, got out his black martial arts clothes and put them on before heading for the gym. It was cool inside and he started with meditation to focus his mind and spirit; then he set about stretching exercises to achieve flexibility and dynamism.

Menn took his posture and leapt into the air, turning as he did so, expressing both attack and defence at the same time, and as he landed he crouched low and turned on a pivot to face the opposite way. He continued with the graceful movements that incorporated decisive punches and thrusts, and saw off invisible assailants. All measured, all executed with poise and control.

When he had finished his routine he did some final stretching exercises turned off the gym lights and went back to his room, satisfied with his commitment. He folded the garments with reverence and stored them in a drawer after which he went for his evening meal.

Chapter 4

BACK in January, the Language Department had held interviews for an English teacher to be Head of International Studies, a department of four that catered for the sizeable number of foreign students who needed assistance with their English, especially to pass the University entrance exam. In March when the Head of Department was away on a school trip and therefore not on hand to influence the outcome, the interviews were rather inconveniently held and a lady was appointed. Come September she duly arrived at the school, but refused to unpack her cases into the staff accommodation that she was given, as if not sure in her mind whether she had arrived with the intention of staying.

Menn was one of a group of Chinese students at the school who needed to attend the classes: some of them were Mandarin speakers whilst others like Menn spoke Hong Kong Cantonese – they shared a common set of written characters but a different spoken language. The issues they faced speaking English were very much in common, from pronunciation of illogically spelled words to the need to interpret the world through word concepts rather than logogram images. As the days and weeks went by, Menn was to think that the teaching staff spoke different languages as he encountered different interpretations of procedures in the school.

"Miss," Menn said as he had walked in for the first lesson. "Miss, what books we need? I got dictionary only. I need speak good for university."

Newly-appointed Miss Butcher was a little reserved, or perhaps aloof, and did not really present a warm point of contact.

"I have books for you all. Wait, be patient. They are coming."

However, she seemed to be allergic to herbs, present in so much cuisine. At least, that is what the students were told when the following week she failed to appear for the first three days, phoning in sick as a result of a reaction to Basil. Work had been set over the phone, and the students effectively taught themselves.

To the cover teacher Menn repeatedly said: "In Hong Kong in my school, teacher come to class and teach. And students come to class and be quiet to study. In my Math class here, always plenty noise and also many times no teacher. Here in English also no teacher. Good we Chinese, and know how be quiet and study."

With which he excused himself from the

classroom and took himself off to the library to study by himself. But the library was full of the students that were injured and not able to do games: it was the easiest option for the games staff and the least desirable for the librarian. Librarians train to manage books, not recalcitrant students with no great interest in reading and no wish to be doing homework either. So it was noisy, and Menn removed himself to his room in the boarding house to study, even though that was frowned upon.

So it was that September slipped by with no teacher much of the time, and no Lantern Festival at all for the Chinese students.

OCTOBER

"When the government is non-invasive, the people are pure and simple.
When the government is intrusive, the people are lacking and wanting."
Lao Tsu
(604 BC – 531 BC)

Chapter 5

THE HMD put his overnight requirements in a valise, and headed off to the Management Training seminar for Aspirant Deputy Heads Designate and Newly-Appointed Headmasters. It was being held in a hotel in London, that had at its disposal a conference room, with the usual audio-visual facilities, a small gym with splash pool, and most important of all, a large bar.

Delegates reported to Reception on arrival and having left their belongings in their rooms, assembled in the bar before taking their random places in the tiered seats of the conference room. HMD had taken advantage of the free introductory drink, and bought a further pint to chase it down. Although the conference room was clearly purpose-built, being an interior room, either the air-conditioning was on and it was cold, or it was off and it was stuffy.

The air-con was off because it always made enough background noise to be intrusive; the ceiling-mounted projector and the electronic whiteboard conspired with the presence of eighty bodies to make the room hot and stuffy; actually, very hot and very stuffy, rather like some of the participants.

"Ladies and Gentlemen, welcome to the seminar. We rather wanted to pick up the lead from the well-established series of books, and call this School Management for Dummies, but felt you might not attend."

A ripple of laughter paid tribute to his joke and broke the ice, though HMD smiled only politely. Arguably the ice was melting of its own accord in the warmth of the room. The presenter continued with the formalities of what to do in case of an emergency, and went over the general timings for the day before launching into the first item on the programme.

"The first lesson to learn on becoming Headmaster is that you have to change your perspective. You remember when you were a classroom teacher, pumping out the information to the kids: I bet there is not a single one of you who did not look at the Senior Management Team and think to yourself: 'If they weren't here, what real difference would it make?'

"Ok, we need a timetable and someone has to drive that, but it is often passed down to one of the staff to do. And you remember all the emails arriving demanding information, data, response, attendance and so on, generated by SMT?

And as you set to teaching your classes you thought: 'For goodness sake - these are not helping the children to learn in the slightest; in fact they are taking up my valuable time reading them when I should be looking at how best to address the students' learning'."

The presenter felt that murmur of recognition from the previous roles of these Aspirants keen to get out of the classroom.

"Well, time to change your perspective, because you are entrusted with the day-to-day running of the school, and obviously you will work hard and have to justify yourselves to your seniors, Department of Education or Board of Governors. And it is you and your team that generate all these emails demanding information and attendance because obviously you need to crunch all of it, and define policy on the back of that."

He went on to observe that the point of resistance, therefore, was the staffroom and its members, reluctant to take on more work on the basis that they had enough already and there weren't enough hours in the day.

"So, Ladies and Gentlemen, you need some strategies to be able to confront the resistance and to tackle the more challenging members of staff. It is no longer challenging pupils, it is challenging teachers."

A corporate grin spread around the room as they briefly but clearly saw both sides of the fence; a little bit like the astro-physicists of today who are in the privileged position of seeing backwards in time to the big bang and forwards to see the big expansion. Actually, of course, only a very, very little bit like such an astrophysicist, but so imbued with their own self-importance were some of the delegates, that they felt thus empowered.

"OK, first strategy. You are giving some bad news to one of your staff. You know they don't support you, don't like you, don't suit you; they are a nuisance to what you are doing. You know the sort. It may be that they are right in what they say, but that is not the point. You are trying to get yes-men around you, not no-men, right? Well, I'll wager that you all thought Black Friday was an American term for October sales, when they celebrate Thanksgiving; or simply that every so often you see stores advertising Black Friday and its price reductions.

Well, here is the management Black Friday variant. You send out the bad news email or snail mail letter to arrive on a Friday, ideally the Friday immediately before half-term or end of term! It's great, because they can't get to you until Monday at the earliest, a week on Monday if it is half-term, and a month on Monday if it is the end of term. The recipient can stew in his or her own juices initially and then reduce to a simmer and cool down to room-temperature by the time contact is next made."

For good measure, the presenter then invited delegates to quickly discuss the strategy with their neighbours to see what they thought. He paused for a while, listening to the murmurs before continuing.

"Everybody happy with that one? Excellent, so let's have a look at one more before we adjourn. I call this one APHC, and it is your trump card to play in virtually any and every situation. This may be a true call, or it may be the bluff that you need to rattle the member of staff, or even have them confess to something that you were not expecting!

"A Parent Has Complained. How easy is that! Call the member of staff in and take him or her to task and say 'A parent has complained'. If a parent has indeed complained, so much the better. If a parent has not complained, it makes no difference. If challenged, you simply respond: "I can't tell you who it is", which of course could be absolutely true if no parent has complained - you cannot possibly tell who it was if there was no-one. However, it goes beyond that, because it is 100% likely that at some point, somewhere in the world, it is true that a parent has complained. Simply make the statement vague and general and non-specific."

He paused as the power of the tool became apparent to all. Then he led the delegates on to the other items of the seminar, looking at legal liabilities of schools, and the extent of Child Protection issues; preparation for inspections; league tables.

Lunch came and went, a brief adjournment for a finger buffet to be taken back to the seats and consumed as a working lunch, a sure-fire way of getting indigestion and no down-time. But, schedules are schedules, and time is at a premium. The atmosphere in the room became thicker still, and HMD from the school had taken in all he needed for the moment: on his notepad he had written 'BF (Black Friday) and APHC (A Parent Has Complained)'. So he settled back into his chair and made no pretence about closing his eyes, perhaps hoping to give the impression of intense concentration. Thus it was that he slipped into slumber mode, much like his electronic notebook did, awakening only when the applause of the delegates greeted the penultimate presentation. HMD promptly started clapping, declaring all that he had slept through to be most interesting indeed and well worth attending.

Their homework for the evening was contained in a one page handout: a scenario typical of school life with a problem that needed to be resolved. And would delegates please give consideration to it for the 10 o'clock session the following day, when they would be put into groups to discuss and report back.

"To conclude today's presentations I would like to end on a lighter, but never the less for that salient note. May I introduce to you Peter Mandini, who is a professional magician. I will let him talk you through the points that he adds to this seminar. Peter."

Peter Mandini stepped forward, looking just like everyone else in the room. That is to say that he was not wearing a magician's top hat, tails and a walking cane: he was wearing a dark suit that might fit funerals and undertakers, and trousers that rose up over the socks as he sat down on a chair in the middle of the stage.

"Ladies and Gentlemen. I am not going to take up too much time at this end of the day, but it seems that you and I are often in the same line of business. In order to carry out my tricks I have to confuse my audience, I have to mislead them, I have to deceive them. I have to create an illusion. And it is not so very difficult, because people want to believe the impossible, they want things to be the way they want them to be, they want to have faith that I can achieve their hopes whether for success or failure. When I cut the lady in half, one part of the audience hopes I can achieve the illusion and the other part of the audience hopes I will fail. And then there is the part that hopes that I really do cut the lady in half and have a bit of a problem on my hands! It is all down to window dressing, smoke and mirrors, and fundamental superstitions."

He held out a flat-pack cardboard box to a member of the audience to check and confirm that it was empty. He took it back, showed it one more time and put it down on the floor. He walked all over it, before asking another member of the audience to assemble the box.

"If I told you that I was going to make a horse come out of the box, you might just not believe me, and I might just not be able to achieve it. David Livingstone might be able to do it on TV. But if I tell you I can make a chicken come out of that empty box, you accept that is possible from the point of view of size but unlikely since I showed the box to be empty. In other words, it has to be largely believable, but stretching the credibility."

With which he put his hand into the box, and brought out a fluffy yellow chick.

"Smoke and mirrors, Ladies and Gentlemen. Smoke and mirrors. But not a mirror to be seen, nor waft of smoke to detect. Let it be."

As the applause greeted the presentation, so the delegates rose from their seats and prepared to depart. HMD headed straight for the bar, and thought to himself how he could do with a bar back at the school, and made a mental note to have one installed as soon as he was installed himself. He espied Caroline coming in, and stood up to greet her. She was Deputy at a school in London, and their paths crossed on these training sessions and on conferences.

"Hi, how are you? What did you think about all of that?"

She smiled warmly and said how much she had enjoyed it, but wasn't that sure about some of the proposed deception.

"Yeah, I know; just might come in handy one day, who knows! What can I get you to drink?"

She declined, and said that she really wanted to go and have a shower and change into something a bit more relaxed. But that she would love to have a drink afterwards, at dinner.

HMD acknowledged, said he looked forward to it, and wondered if she needed her back rubbed.

Caroline reappeared suitably refreshed, and made her way to the corner where HMD was seated. He saw her approach, got up and giving her a hug, asked what she would like to drink.

"Well, you know me, a G&T please, nothing fancy, just a bit of lemon, lime if they have got it."

He brought the drink from the bar, and handing it to her, sat down on the leather sofa, his leg just brushing hers.

"Cheers," he said. "And many more of them."

"Cheers to that," she said, and as they touched glasses so they held each other's gaze, just a tad too long perhaps.

They washed the steak down with a bottle of Chateauneuf-du-Pape 2010, and his sighs of contentment turned increasingly into more raucous laughter as he poured yet another glass each. She had always felt somehow entranced and in awe at his stories of prowess as a younger man when he played sport at county level. Now she was perhaps wondering how relevant that was to where he was at.

Having finished the meal, he led her outside onto the terrace, glasses of wine in hand, and they made another toast.

"To the future, by hook or by crook!" he said.

"By hook or by crook!" she replied.

And he leaned forward and kissed her under the full light of the moon.

"Is it a new moon, or a full moon?" he asked. "I never know."

"Pretty sure it's a full moon, 'cos you can't see much

of new moons." And she giggled a bit as she drank some more wine.

"Ah, well here's to that. Shall we go upstairs?"

So they made their way up the balustrade stairway and just happened to be both on the same floor. The moon looked down impassively but even so witnessing all.

HMD was up promptly in the morning, and took himself off to the hotel gym. Commendably, he liked to keep fit, and it went with the background he came from. He worked his way around a small selection of machines, and finished off studying himself in the full-length mirror. He enjoyed seeing himself projected back at himself. He looked up at the clock and saw that it was only seven. Breakfast at nine, so the better part of two hours to get the homework done!

Back in his room, he thought about the seminar points from the day before, thought about the time spent with Caroline, and finally gave thought to the scenario they had been given:

"A member of staff is seeing the wife of one of the governors; it would seem that both spouses are unaware of the liaison. How might you seek to address the situation?"

HMD had learned on the sports pitch to

react to the development in the game without thinking first: a slightly more peaceful way of firing from the hip. So it was always a knee-jerk reaction, and always physical. So it was with his approach to the scenario, not much conscious thought: a rush of adrenalin, a lot of tackle hard, take out the threat and job done. Pleased with his rapid take on the issue, he went down to breakfast and got ready for the ten o'clock session. He was a big man with a perpetual smile that masked his agendas and intentions, so he looked in the mirror and the image in the mirror smiled reassuringly back at him.

The delegates were formed up into syndicate groups and sent off into different areas to talk through the scenario and their options. HMD's syndicate comprised a couple of Deputies from different types of schools, some from the independent sector, others from academies newly formed. He sat and listened to the options put forward, occasionally nodding his head, rather more often shaking it. It then came round to him.

HMD however was not putting forward an option: he was putting forward **the** solution. He presented his reaction to the situation as a "go left, get him down, knee on the neck" move. The reaction of the other delegates was one of baffled confusion, and principled objections to what had been said. HMD became uneasy, he felt a self-protective red cloud start to come over him; he felt his heart rate go up, and his face began to glow with the increased flow of blood.

He felt uncomfortable and leapt up, grabbing the hand of the nominated syndicate leader and said with anger:

"OK, we can talk about it later; I've got to take a call."

With that he stormed off to the bar. He felt better for a drink, though it fuelled his aggression. The syndicates had started to stand down for a coffee break when HMD went back to them. He went up to one of the ladies from the group and said:

"You could see what I was saying, couldn't you? You thought they were wrong." She looked at him bewildered and said: "I don't know what you are talking about."

He went up to another and confronted him, a young teacher not yet a Deputy Head even, but ever hopeful. HMD was considerably bigger than he, and he backed him into a corner, leant over him and encroaching into his personal space tackled him with:

"You thought they were wrong, didn't you; you could see my solution, couldn't you?" They were not even rhetorical questions. They were statements to be accepted, like a player yielding to a tackle and falling to the ground.

"I don't understand what you are saying," he said, somewhat unnerved by the physical presence of HMD bearing down on him.

"Well, someone else said that they understood. And that they thought my solution was best."

He pulled away, went back to his room, grabbed his things, jumped into his car and returned home to his family.

Chapter 6

Meanwhile, the Fire Inspector had arrived to carry out a fire risk assessment, and he was busily going about fire alarms and smoke detectors to confirm that all was in order.

Menn was in Louise Arnold's Drama and Media lesson when the Fire Inspector called. He knocked on the door and put his head inside:

"Sorry to disturb, I'm just doing my rounds looking at fire alarms – any issues you are aware of?

"Only that there is no fire alarm, which is what we said last year," said June. "We are not connected to the main fire alarm circuit, and I guess it would be good if we were, because we cannot hear the alarm when it goes off for fire practices."

"Yes, I remember; I did make a recommendation last time but that's as far as my remit goes. It's down to the people at the top after that. Anyway, do you know where the Fire Assembly Point is?"

Teacher and students, less Menn who was too new to know, pointed through the window towards the front of the school, just beyond the Library. Menn looked where they were all indicating, and made a mental note, just in case.

"Is Assembly Point for everyone?"

"No, Menn, only for these classrooms and the library. Everyone else goes the other way." At that, the Fire Inspector withdrew, and the class continued.

The following week, the Science experiment produced rather more gas than desirable, and it was minutes only before the smoke detector sensed the anomaly and set off the alarm. This was echoed throughout the buildings and classes started to evacuate the rooms, heading for the back of the school.

Menn, however, and the rest of his class were deeply immersed in a video on Staging and Lighting, and were blissfully unaware of the emergency evacuation taking place, since their classroom was not connected to the main circuit and did not have a fire alarm.

It was only the intervention of Ruddles, the Estate Manager, and one of the Deputy Heads that alerted the small suite of classrooms:

"Why aren't you moving? It's a fire alarm. Get yourselves moving. Come on. You are going to get caught"

The teachers faced their classes, and re-installed some calm to the situation that was being inflamed by over-enthusiasm and excess drama. The pupils in the room were buzzing with excitement and nervous energy.

"OK, guys. Settle down and listen in." She switched off the video that they were watching and turned to the Deputy Head who was hovering at the open door:

"Please step into the room and close the door. I believe that the advice in case of fire is to keep all doors and windows shut." The bustle of noise in the classroom subsided.

"Peter, please close the window beside you. Everyone please be quiet, and stand up."

She turned to the Deputy Head and said: "Can you hear the fire alarm when you are in here?" The ringing was conspicuous by its absence. "And we have commented on this before, repeatedly."

Ruddles had opened the door and come in to speed up the evacuation, bellowing: "Get out, now." The students started to get spooked again.

To the class the teacher said calmly: "Settle down. Leave your things where they are, turn left out of the door and form up in front of the library. First row, off you go."

"No, no!" shouted Ruddles, "They have to go round the back onto the car park."

"But that involves going past the Science Labs, where I am guessing the alleged fire is raging. The notices in this corridor and the statement in the Policy Document state quite clearly that our Assembly Point is in front of the Library, in the opposite direction."

Menn heard and saw this disconnect with disbelief, and simply followed the file of exiting students. They were duly force-marched past the culprit Science Laboratory whose strident alarms rang out danger, but were given scant serious attention beyond joyful evacuation by the Science classes.

Chapter 7

THE staff meeting that was called was not a staff meeting in the normal sense – it was not a forum for complaints and criticism from moaning teachers: far too radical and dangerous. Rather was it a forum for the HMD to brief the staff in an uncompromising transmit only mode. In this instance, however, it was a valuable moment since there was a message for everyone.

"Good morning everybody. Firstly the Fire Alert yesterday. It was not a practice, but a very real evacuation due to an incident in the Science Block. It was orderly and rapid, though we have identified some issues that will be looked into.

Secondly, we have been advised that there will be a brief inspection after half-term, because in the previous one last year there were issues with boarding arrangements, and the inspectors wish to confirm that improvements have been made. However, they will take the opportunity to inspect general teaching in the classroom as well, though it will not feature in their report."

"So, how many lessons can we expect them to want to visit informally? And do we have to produce a lesson plan?"

"Short answer is probably one class per department and yes to the lesson plan – but you should be producing those any way."

Julie from the Maths Department wondered if her dentist had to write up a detailed plan for every patient who came in and needed treatment. And then shuddered at the thought that went through everybody's head that half term would be spent producing lavish plans.

As autumn colours bedecked the trees, so half-term approached and finally arrived. The inevitable holiday homework had been set for the public exam students to consider at least, if not to do with much enthusiasm; teachers' tables were cleared and final bits of marking dealt with; and buses arrived to take eager students away for ten days, seen off the premises by Suits overseeing but not adding much to the discipline at the crossing.

"You off anywhere?" one teacher voice asked.

"No, just chilling at home."

"Yep, we're taking a group from the French classes across the Channel for a visit."

"Don't forget the Inspection preparation."

With which they got into their cars and

followed the flight of the buses out of the campus. Menn was going to spend the half-term with a host family arranged by the placing agency. He had packed his case with his martial arts clothing amongst the contents and boarded the taxi that arrived to take him away for the duration. The moon was just showing in the distance, growing steadily and shining clearly as it looked down on the proceedings.

NOVEMBER

"If you do not change direction, you may end up where you are headed"
Lao Tsu
(604 BC – 531 BC)

Chapter 8

AFTER the half-term break, once Menn had settled in and learned how the school worked, he was made a prefect. It was a challenge because of the cultural differences, but he held his own in the early stages and exercised his authority over the dinner queues, the tuck shop queues and the end of day coach queues.

Every week there was a Prefects' meeting in HMD's office in the absence of an HM. The group of senior students in the school gathered along with the appointed Heads of School, a boy and a girl in the Upper Sixth who seemed to have the maturity to be figure head leaders to the other prefects.

"Good afternoon to you all, thank you for coming: a few house-keeping points for you all to take on board …," and HMD went through a list of up-coming events and Prefect commitments. Then he turned his attention to school uniform and the need to ensure that pupils were correctly dressed, and for the Prefects to set a good example.

"Peer Listeners is the next thing to deal with," HMD continued. "We need to form up a new team of Peer Listeners. The aim is to hear any grievances from the lower parts of the school, bullying, home issues that are causing upsets – all those sorts of things.

And also any issues with the school that are not being raised at School Council – we need to know what is going on in the school and you Prefects and the Peer Listeners are my eyes and ears around the place. Any information you can bring to identify dissatisfaction and uncooperative people makes my job easier, and I shall be over the moon for your assistance."

As the meeting finished and the Prefects departed, Menn thought on HMD's words, and wondered why he thought he would be over the moon, when we must all know our place is under the moon. He went back to his room to get ready for the next classes he was due to attend. Whilst in some respects it mattered little if he attended or not since he was not studying for exams, it did matter to Menn personally for he had a mission in his heart to gain maximum benefit from his year and end up with fluency in his English to match his mastery of Chinese. The House Master saw him, and asked how the meeting had gone. He listened as Menn related what HMD had told them and he said to Menn:

"You know, Menn, in life you discover that you cannot have too much information, and my wife Kate would say that you need to listen carefully to everything and store it in your memory so that you can make better sense of the world and its societies."

Menn looked at him and said: "I will make sure to listen well. In Chinese we say: **If you wish to know the mind of a man, listen to his words**."

The Housemaster nodded and said that they were wise words. Then Menn said: "Also we say in Chinese: **When a woman talks to you smile but do not listen**."

The Housemaster burst out laughing and did a high five with Menn, who set off for his classes, thinking how much listening and how much smiling he needed to do. He felt himself like a heavenly body in orbit that not only looked down on but listened up to the earth.

Chapter 9

HEAD of Outdoor Pursuits had taken up his post in September a year ago, and set out to make the Department become a centre for excellence. To that end he had secured the services of a Paramedic to deliver First Aid Training to the students that signed up for the Duke of Edinburgh Scheme, or went off at weekends for Adventure Activities.

The Paramedic was excellent, not least of all because he impressed the students when he arrived in a white car marked Medic, with blue lights on the top, and he wore his working green uniform. His knowledge was current, and he brought with him manikins on which to practise CPR, and make-up to simulate wounds on the students. Head of Outdoor Pursuits and the Paramedic set up realistic scenarios around the campus, and once they had done their training, groups of students 'came upon' the incident and took enthusiastic action. It was a salutary lesson to watch their reactions to situations beyond their years and hopefully forever beyond their experiences in life.

"Guys, do not all gather round the same casualty like Year Sevens around a football. One of you attend one casualty, the others look around for where else needs attention. And cut the noise down."

They slowly got the idea and once they were doing it mostly well the practice was brought to a temporary halt.

"Over here, people. Well done – you started to think wide. Now I am going to give you some important pointers for these situations. First I am going to nominate one of you as the officer In Charge, the IC, and he or she does not get involved in the treatment directly. He or she stands back, ideally somewhere in the middle in order to be able to see what is happening around. The IC will give direction, as the manager. Secondly, you need to prioritise the needs – someone who has fainted is not as needy as someone who is bleeding profusely from a wound; the casualty who is choking is more critical than the one who is wandering round incoherent.

Menn, let's make you the IC; the remainder of you are in support of Menn, and you have to listen to what Menn tells you to do, but help him with your information and assessments. Don't all bunch on the same casualty, do keep all the chat down."

"Menn, over here for a briefing." The paramedic spoke quietly to Menn about his role, and explained to him how to do it. In Hong Kong, Menn had already had experience of this in the Scouts, and knew a lot about First Aid and Expeditions from many a training session in the New Territories. Furthermore, he had taken part in Civil Defence Training in the summer before coming across to England and he had impressed his course instructors with his enthusiasm and quick learning. So he nodded wisely as he took on board the requirement to manage a group of enthusiastic youngsters who needed leadership and direction. The scenario was realistic: a vehicle had been parked up, with three casualties inside and outside - a road traffic accident that might have been a collision with a tree, a hijacking or a bomb going off.

Menn rose to the occasion, and held everyone back as he carried out drills inside his head that he had learned: check for petrol leaking from the hot engine; check for anyone lying in ambush nearby; check for any obvious wires and explosive devices. Better to lose *them* than all of *us*, he remembered his instructor saying. Once he was satisfied that there were no dangers, he sent two First Aiders over to a casualty who was threshing around, with instructions to calm him, contain him and attend to him; one of the two was then to return to Menn for further instructions. A further two were dispatched to the car where the driver was hunched over the steering wheel, moaning quietly; and two were sent to the final casualty who seemed to have gone through the windscreen and lay in the grass, a realistic gash to his thigh showing itself through his torn trousers.

The Paramedic congratulated Menn on his management of the situation, and the six First Aiders for their skills in dealing with the casualties.

"Sir, I good to save life and make plans for organise helpers. Maybe if I join in Army, can do good job. Can take life also."

"Menn, great effort," said the Head of Outdoor Pursuits. "Well done. You might make a good soldier, maybe even officer in your army. But please do not be taking my life!"

"Sir, no Sir. You good man. Only take bad men!" Menn grinned as he looked at the two adults.

Chapter 10

BACK in September, as the Head of Outdoor Pursuits and the Paramedic made their way back to the staffroom after some First Aid training, the Paramedic asked: "Have you got a defibrillator in the school, 'cos I haven't seen one?"

"Nope, I asked the nurse in the sick bay, and she said she had asked for one but was told that it was going to cost too much and it wasn't in her budget."

"So how about I get you one?"

"Sounds great, and can you then do a series of defibrillator training sessions for us? I realise that they are reasonably self-explanatory, but the session we had when we did First Aid refresher just before the beginning of term was sketchy."

So it was that the following week the Paramedic turned up with the training defibrillator and students started to gain the confidence to access the machine and feel comfortable with the potential need to use it.

"I have cleared it with my boss," he said, "and I will bring the active defibrillator for you next week."

This he duly did and it was then handed on to the nurse who in turn put it into a cupboard pending a decision on siting the machine. This particular matter was passed up to HMD and to Estates Manager, both of whom took the line that the machine should be kept away from children lest they vandalise it. And so it was that it remained in the cupboard gathering dust and losing battery power for many weeks to come.

In October the Paramedic said that in order to maintain the function of the machine, he needed to check the battery and take appropriate action, and asked when it would be mounted. The nurse explained the situation, and the machine gathered still more dust.

It was to be a further month and much prodding on the part of the Head of Outdoor Pursuits before a proposal was made that it be sited at the Medical Centre, but on the inside of the door.

"But the youngsters are not allowed into the Medical Centre, and what happens if access is needed after-hours and the Medical Centre is locked?" asked Head of Outdoor Pursuits.

So the machine gathered more dust, and the Paramedic threatened to take the machine away to appease his boss unless it was sited appropriately. Finally the luminaries worked it out, and had it sited at the Medical Centre on the outside of the door so it was accessible at all times. Unsurprisingly, no-one vandalised it.

But as the weeks had passed, all students who were taking part in the Outdoor Pursuits activities had had the opportunity to learn how to use the training machine, as did anyone else who wanted the practice, although surprisingly few took up the option.

It was Menn who was first to use it towards the end of the month, when the weather had turned, and darkness set in early. One of the Science Department teachers was hurrying along the walkway to get to a meeting, when he slid on the wet concrete which was as slippery as ice. He held aloft the laptop that he was carrying and sacrificed his own welfare for the sake of the electronic god. But, on reaching the hard surface, he fell awkwardly and twisted his leg against the natural direction of the joint, feeling and hearing the crack. He went into shock and had lost consciousness by the time Menn, who was the sole other person around, reached him from the far end. He saw the leg at an unnatural angle, but ignored it, rather more concerned as he was with the unconscious state of the teacher.

"Sir, Sir - can you hear me?" and he gently shook his shoulders to get a response. There being no response, Menn leaned over and opened his mouth, but there seemed to be no obstruction, so he checked his breathing, which was shallow if at all. Menn looked around and shouted for help, but no-one was in sight. He dashed to the Medical Centre door, and grabbed the defibrillator. Conscious of the passing of time, he unbuttoned the shirt, switched on the machine, got the pads out of the sealed pack, and stuck one high on the top of the right hand side of the chest, and the other on the other side, below his left armpit.

He waited for the instructions. The machine identified the need, and Menn heard the recorded instruction to shock, so he pressed the shock button, and then set about giving compressions, and waited for a further instruction. At last another student came upon the situation, and Menn told him to go get a teacher, from a meeting if necessary, and to call an ambulance. The machine demanded a further shock, which Menn dutifully delivered.

Two members of staff came running and took over the care of the limp body, and Menn stood back, adrenalin starting to course through his body. He took himself off to his room, and lay down on his bed and fell fast asleep. Later his Housemaster came to see him, to check how he was, and to tell him that the ambulance had come and taken the teacher to hospital, no further details.

Chapter 11

MENN was very much the product of his environment during his up-bringing and education in Hong Kong. For those parents in Asia who understood the issues, and that was the majority, education was the master key to progress, because the alternatives of hawking, driving taxis or sleeping under bridges were unpalatable. So it was that parents pushed their children hard to succeed in public exams, and expected their offspring to get the results needed to get closer to the desired outcome.

So Menn had attended extra classes after school to push him relentlessly onwards to outshine his peers, and he was as adept at using the abacus to calculate as the electronic calculator. Now being at this school to improve his English, he attended many subjects merely to get exposure to the language. The A Level Maths class was not difficult for him in terms of content, but challenging at times in terms of English.

"Miss, how you say this?" and he wrote '¾' on a piece of paper. "In Cantonese we say 'out of four parts take three'. What you say in English?"

"Three quarters, Menn."

"I not see that, Miss. I see in my head 'out of four parts take three'. I not see 'three quarters'. Chinese all good in Maths 'cos Chinese numbers good"

There was a giggle from the other students in the class, all local students who struggled with the Maths and not the English. But Menn was not perturbed, for he had already taken the exam, and preferred to do calculations in Cantonese, because the language for the number system was simpler, shorter and quicker. Nonetheless, he was determined to hold his own in expressing the concepts in English.

He liked Maths, and planned to go on to study Computer Studies and Maths at university, so it was valuable for him to revise the subject and interface with the relevant language. So it was a source of frustration for him on the occasions when the maths teacher did not turn up for the class due to over-involvement with other important matters, which was not infrequent and increasingly more common. Hence sometimes it fell to him to help the others with the mathematical functions, and bit by bit they helped him with the expression of the processes in English.

On the occasions the Maths teacher did not come, caught up in her other conflicting duties, another teacher came in to supervise the lesson, but was never a Maths specialist, and Menn felt a degree of anger rise within him as the term progressed, wondering how this system worked, and sympathised with the plight of the students.

"How you guys can learn the Maths properly if no teacher comes?"

"It's not good, Menn; and one of this group now does not come to class on account of the teacher not coming: he goes home with a friend and they work together to do the Maths. We have complained, but nothing happens because the teacher is also a Deputy Head. Boring!"

"But in good schools in Hong Kong teachers are always in class, and students be very quiet. Why there is so noisy and no learning in class here sometimes?"

"I think you should stay in Hong Kong, Menn. Sounds better than here!"

"Because I need experience of UK and need to study here to go to University. Also Agency find this place, so should be good. Just need teacher."

Chapter 12

IT was the centenary commemoration of the end of World War One, and the school was busily making preparations to mark the occasion with a service on the Sunday, which coincided with the 11th day of the eleventh month. There was to be a service with the choir rightly taking pride of place: its renditions were the product of many hours of practice and were a testament to the efforts by staff and by students.

Menn had seen the Remembrance Service in Hong Kong the previous year. Almost a post-colonial anomaly, there was a service organised by the Hong Kong branch of the Royal British Legion at a Cenotaph constructed in 1923 in Central, an exact replica of the Cenotaph in London. Having lost his own father during the Japanese occupation of Hong Kong in the war Menn's father had attended services there prior to hand-over in 1997, and long after hand-over he had taken his son Menn to pay respects when he was old enough to understand.

Menn had watched the Hong Kong Police band and Youth Groups as they paraded in uniform in front of the Cenotaph where the government representatives laid wreaths. He had been moved by the gathering of Europeans, Chinese and Moslems who came together to remember those who had been lost, and who wore their poppy with pride.

As the 100th anniversary approached, mention was made over successive school assemblies of the devastating loss of life. One man died every five seconds in the Battle of the Somme, 20,000 on day one; 700,000 UK deaths in the war itself: the numbers were numbing and Menn thought of the grandfather he had never known.

"Sir," he said to his Housemaster one evening. "In Hong Kong I have been to Cenotaph in Central and seen the Remembrance Parade; last year we went. My grandfather died Christmas Day 1941 when Japanese invaded. He working in hospital, and Japanese Imperial Army kill many."

"Menn, I am sorry. They were difficult days. It will be a good service here to remember everyone."

"Sir, is possible go to Cenotaph in London?"

"I don't know, Menn. I will ask."

Menn went off to his room and looked up the details of the London service, establishing where it was exactly and how to get there. The Housemaster remembered that Louise Arnold in the Drama Department had said over morning coffee a few weeks back that her brother, serving with the army in Kent, was going to be attending the laying of a wreath at the Gurkha Statue in Whitehall. Louise wanted to attend the event and was going to ask leave to go and watch.

Although that was taking place the day before Remembrance Sunday, she planned to stay on in London to watch the ceremony at the Cenotaph.

The Housemaster sought Louise out and ascertained that she had been given permission, and he formulated the makings of a plan for Menn to be escorted by her. Armed with the solution, he asked the question and was pleasantly surprised to be told that Menn could indeed go to the Cenotaph ceremony, in the company of Louise.

So it was, then, that on 11th November, Louise met Menn off the train at Charing Cross, and they made their way to the Cenotaph. They met up with Louise's brother at the security point, and having shown to be innocent such bags as they carried, they jostled through the crowds towards the monument. Menn looked with respectful wonderment as the Guard's band marched past:

"Miss, is so great. I seen in Hong Kong and it is good, but this is amazing. Thank you for bring me."

"You are welcome, Menn," and raising her hand she did a high five with him as her brother, in uniform with medals won in Afghanistan, took a photo on his phone. Her brother in turn put out his hand to shake hands with Menn.

"All brave men," said Menn. "Like my grandfather long time ago."

They watched as Prince Harry laid a wreath on behalf of the Queen, his grandmother, who was watching from the Foreign and Commonwealth balcony opposite the Cenotaph. Menn took photographs to send back to Hong Kong for his family to share: they having attended the parallel act of remembrance some seven hours earlier, had sent Menn images from Central and he was delighted to bring the two ceremonies together.

He asked Louise's brother to forward him the picture of high fives with Louise, and once air-dropped he sent that to Hong Kong as well, with the caption: "Kind teacher Miss Arnold take me to London for Cenotaph."

With a few rapid and deft moves on his phone, Menn posted the same photo on his Facebook page, shared and liked in Hong Kong as much as amongst new contacts in England.

DECEMBER

"The truth is not always beautiful,
Nor beautiful words the truth"
Lao Tzu
(604 BC – 531 BC)

Chapter 12

REHEARSALS for the play had been taking place for many weeks. Taking part in the school play was a real opportunity for those who might be less strong academically to shine in an area that was not illuminated solely by the spaghetti alphabet of A, B and Cs, or the lottery of 9, 8 and 7s, which in its turn offered the possibility of trumping previous generations of proud holders of a 9 with the inflationary introduction of a 10.

Louise was the sole member of her drama department, so had no-one to delegate to, and no-one to answer to either, other than herself. And so it was that she consulted herself as to which dramatic production to offer next at the beginning of term, invited students from Years 9 upwards to offer their services, whether treading the boards or being in support.

"Now, who will make a good pig?" she thought. "And who shall I put as Farmer Jones?"; for she had settled on Animal Farm, feeling that George Orwell had great insight into the warped dynamics of social systems, and this needed airing for the education and entertainment of this century's young.

Having cast the parts, and given lines to be learned by some for whom learning their home address was a challenge due to their dyslexia, Louise was heartened at the way it was going, on yet another Sunday spent in the drama hall.

"Harry, you need to make a more emphatic entrance: you may well be a pig, but you are a really important pig because you are challenging the establishment. You are the leader of the down-trodden," she said as she strove to get more impact out of youngsters dealing with issues beyond their years.

"How do you mean, Miss?"

"Feel big, feel important, you are aiming for the top, for a take-over. You know: **I've got something to say, and you are all going to pay heed. I'm a big pig!**"

The scene was dinner in the farm house:

Stage right: Farmer Jones sat at a trestle table with his wife, supping copious glasses of wine and then spirits, making more and more grunting noises as he became more and more full of himself and alcohol.

Enter stage left: Pig and Donkey, who approach a window Centre stage and look through it at the increasing debauchery within.

"But they are supposed to be feeding the animals and putting them to bed," said Donkey. "It is their responsibility to care for us."

"Indeed it is, Donkey. But they have no care for other than themselves. Just listen to the noises they are making - they have become inarticulate and grunt gutturally as they gorge."

"But, Pig - are we not now all equal, and entitled to our share of the food and a barn in which to sleep?"

"Indeed we are all equal, Donkey. It's just that some are more equal than others."

With that the pair of them exited Stage Left, accompanied by a belch from Stage Right.

The Dress Rehearsal many weeks later was not bad at all, apart from the fact that when Louise arrived at the Hall, she found it securely locked up for the afternoon. She did not have a key herself, because the Head of Estates had decided that it was a security risk to issue keys or to leave the Hall unlocked and unattended. For a singularly unimaginative person, Ruddles was imbued with a great image of self-importance and had that attitude that is identified by psychometric tests filtering applicants for Traffic Wardens and other such rule-bound bureaucratic posts. The fact that the office of one of the Deputy Heads was directly facing the Hall, and that the Deputy in question seemed always to be in his office, did not hold any sway.

"Ah", she said to the cast who were all gathered round the locked door rather expectantly. "Unfortunately, we seem to be locked out. Which is a bit of a pain because only this morning I double checked with the system that the Hall was still available to us for the Dress Rehearsal and that it would be left open for two o'clock. Wait here, back in a minute".

So Louise went off in search of Ruddles, who was in his office having a meeting with some of the ground staff. She knocked on the door and stood back so that she might be seen through the glass pane. He looked up but continued with his meeting. So she knocked again, as politely as one may knock on a door.

Ruddles scowled at her, went still redder in the face than he normally was, and went to the door.

"Can't you see, I'm in a meeting", he expostulated and shut the door in her face.

"Uhhm," thought Louise to herself. "What to do now?

Which has greater priority? A jolly important meeting or a jolly important Dress Rehearsal?"

Even as she spent that fraction of time considering the issue, the rain started to fall first lightly then like stair rods.

So she knocked on the door again and smiled most sweetly through the glass; and then opened the door and put her head inside. She was met with a torrent of verbal abuse even as she opened her mouth to speak. She reeled back a bit, like a boxer who has received a blow to the head.

"So sorry to interrupt, but the Hall is inexplicably locked even though I have booked it to be open at two o'clock for the Dress Rehearsal, and as you know, I do not have a key, even though I did suggest it might be a good idea in order not to have to disturb anyone. And it's raining. And the youngsters are all standing outside the locked door, I guess getting wet."

Ruddles lifted himself from his swivel chair and found the key to the Hall. Rather begrudgingly, Louise felt, he handed it to her in a very abrupt fashion.

"I'm having a meeting," he said and shook his head in apparent disbelief at the interruption.

Louise went back to the locked door, and

found her cast sheltering from the rain by holding their scripts over their heads like umbrellas.

"Miss, we're all wet now. It's not fair".

"Sorry, everyone. Not my fault. Life it seems just isn't fair. Some are more equal than others!" said Louise.

A rain drop trickled down the forehead of Pig, glanced off his eye and looked for all the world like a tear.

Once inside, she set about getting the youngsters into their roles, not just recalling the lines, but entering into the spirit of the character as well. They moved with increasing confidence around the boards of the stage, and slowly became the personalities they were embodying.

Chapter 13

THE evening after the Dress Rehearsal was the actual performance, and parents had been invited weeks earlier, doors to open at seven and show to start at seven thirty. Menn had been invited to stand at the door and act as Front of House taking monies, issuing entrance tickets in the form of programmes and guiding guests over to the member of staff offering refreshments in the form of glasses of wine or orange juice. After having steadied the cast down, Louise slipped into the body of the Hall and stood for a moment at the door where Menn was happily busying himself attending to the steady influx of guests.

"Well done, Menn. Thank you," she said. "A good turn-out" She looked at the Reserved Seats at the front allocated to the senior echelons of school staff. "Conspicuously empty", she muttered, and went back-stage to re-join the cast.

"Time, everyone - settle down. Relax, enjoy yourselves. Think big. You know where I am sitting, just at the front to your right if you need a prompt." Louise then pushed through the closed curtains to introduce the play.

"Ladies and Gentlemen, thank you so much ...."

She stopped as the doors opened and an entourage of four, HMD and Deputies, all dressed in their undertaker suits, stepped in and fiddled their way through the half-light to their reserved seats at the front.

Louise waited for the commotion to cease, and started her welcome again, pointing out the fire exits and observing that there would be an interval after the first hour, with the second part being only thirty-five minutes long.

"For those of you who may have forgotten, in Animal Farm, George Orwell addresses events leading to the Russian Revolution in 1917. The animals represent key players in the political and cultural revolution of the time, built upon a cult of personality and enforced by a reign of terror. Look no further than the current world leaders - but I am not here to make contentious statements: I will let George Orwell and the members of the cast do that!

Finally, may I ask you to turn your phones off or put them on silent. Thank you very much - enjoy the play!"

She sat down to applause and the lights fully dimmed as the curtains parted.

George Orwell would have been suitably impressed by the performance of the young cast who acted their little hearts out. The animals became authentically animal and drew the audience into their personae.

Only once, half way through the first half, did a mobile phone go off, just to the right of Louise. She took her eyes off the script and looked sideways to see the HMD holding the offending phone in his hand. It was as she re-found her place in the script that she heard "Line" coming her way from the stage. The drama continued to unfold on the stage until tumultuous clapping greeted the closing of the curtains as the first part came to a close.

There were biscuits available during the interval, and one of the parents dropped half of hers as a fault line developed across it when she bit into it and it fell to the floor. She stooped to recover it but thought better of it as she watched a cockroach scuttle out from the crack between wall and floor and set upon the crumbs. Menn appeared as if from nowhere and he extended a foot and trod on the creature.

When the performance resumed after the interval, Louise noted that the huddle of Suits along from her had departed and not returned. There were no more phone interruptions.

As the curtains closed the audience clapped long and loud, and the cast stepped through to the front and took bows. Louise was brought onto the stage and presented with a bouquet of well-deserved flowers and in her turn extended an arm to the cast and clapped them - one more successful play. But the men in suits were not present to pay any heed.

Long after the audience had gone home with their thespian off-spring in tow, Louise stayed on accompanied by Menn in order to dismantle the stage and earn herself a day off before Monday came round again. The pair of them worked beyond midnight until the task was completed, when she thanked Menn for his help and having ensured he got off to his room she let herself out into the cold night air, catching sight of a slither of moon that looked like the taut D of a bow in an archer's hands.

Chapter 14

WHEN Monday arrived, Louise and every other member of staff were intrigued to receive, among the normal deluge of emails, one that seemed rather out of the ordinary. In the Bursar's office was one Mary, who with several others maintained some of the many accounts that existed for the school. Mary had been poorly and in accordance with the note from her doctor was seeking time off to convalesce, to which end she had phoned her line manager, namely the Bursar, to present her case.

"The doctor has given me a sick note, because I am suffering from the after-effects of the flu that's been going around. As you know, when I was going down with the flu, I came in to get those accounts done that you wanted, and it's all caught up with me now."

"Uhm, I see. Well it's not a particularly convenient moment because the Governors are meeting next week, and they will want to look over the figures for this term." He sucked on his teeth and inhaled deeply before continuing: "You've been off since Thursday now. How much longer are you needing off?"

"Well, as you will see, the doctor has given me a week

off. I don't think it will be any longer, not if I can get the rest I need."

"I'll have to pass it up to HR because you have had so much time off."

So it was that the matter was passed up, along or down, according to one's perspective, to the hands of HR, a large lady with a charming smile and a penchant for firing from the hip, and firing big. So much power at the hands of one so big and with so little judgement that it was fortuitous that she was not Kim Jong-un with finger hovering over the nuclear button.

HR fired up her computer, and calling on her undisputed knowledge of procedure in such cases started to type with relish:

To: Mary Payne
From: HR
Subject: Sick leave

I understand that you have a doctor's note prescribing a further week off work. Since you have already been off work for four days, in accordance with government regulations, we will reduce your pay to SSP (Statutory Sick Pay) £92.05 per week with immediate

**effect. We wish you a speedy
recovery.**

Pleased with the terse, to-the-point tone, she hovered her finger no more than a millisecond over the SEND button before launching the email into cyberspace.

So it was that Louise and a further seventy colleagues in the All Staff Group found the email in their in-boxes, for HR had not checked her co-ordinates before the launch of her intercontinental ballistic missive, a weapon of mass instruction, happily with no warhead attached, at least not this time.

"Poor Mary", a voice was heard in the staff room at morning break, a "prayers" meeting when the HMD addressed everyone. "Paula, I know that Mary is not strictly speaking a member of the staff room, but couldn't we send her a card and a little something to show that we are thinking of her."

Paula was in charge of the Staffroom Fund that all of the teachers in the staffroom were invited to contribute to each term in order to fund leaving presents and cards. In the event, not all teachers actually bothered to make the contribution, though in fairness most did. Hence some staff would leave at some future point well ahead of the curve since they would receive a farewell gift, having made no investment in the scheme.

"Good idea," said Paula, "but I can't really use the Staffroom Fund for that, so I will put an envelope on the table today, and this afternoon when we go home, I will take your contributions, put up a notice to say how much was raised, and buy something appropriate to that value."

"I've had a thought," a voice said from the back. "Maybe you could let us know how much is raised in an email via the All Staff Group."

The games staff was congratulated on the fine turn out on the Saturday for the teams' efforts on the sports pitches, the groundsman was congratulated on preparing the grounds so well, the boarding staff was congratulated on taking their charges to town on Saturday afternoon to go shopping. And so it went on, a thank-you repeated in a vaguely well-meant way to hard-working people, but somehow lacking in sincerity since there were so many of them. Rather akin to Oscar recipients or Miss World finalists thanking everyone including Aunt Mabel for support and help and love etc, etc.

Louise was conspicuously not congratulated on the performance of Animal Farm, during which HMD had left in the interval and not returned.

Chapter 15

IT was Friday, at the end of the same week, the lesson before the end of classes in the afternoon, when one of the under-Deputies went to Louise's classroom just before the last class arrived. He said nothing, made his way to the teacher's table and put an envelope on top of it. She looked surprised at the silent visitor, who was not strong as a manager, and had not a trait of leadership in him. She had opened the envelope and read the brief note before he had time to withdraw.

A complaint has been made that you have ......

She rounded on the figure that was just disappearing through the door, outside of which the next class was starting to form up. She verbally dragged him back into the room, and glowered at him with controlled anger in her eyes:

"How dare you slope into my classroom and slide this onto my table when you know full well that I have a class to teach. Do you think that it enhances my teaching, helps the children to learn in a relaxed environment? You have got about as much management skill as a hamster in a wheel, and as much tact and diplomacy as a ferret."

With which she opened the door to him, saw him out, and invited the children to come inside in a quiet and orderly manner. She had fun with them all, and then set up the homework for the weekend; as the clock moved to show four o'clock she had them stand quietly, wished them all a good weekend and saw them out.

Then she turned her attentions to the letter. It was lacking in any specific detail other than to say that a complaint had been made concerning an inappropriate relationship with a Sixth Former and that there was to be a meeting on Monday to discuss.

Black Friday bad news tactics: so much for the weekend then, the first with no involvement in the play accounting for her time and energy. It was the anticipation of the meeting rather than any actual guilt or concern; a bit like waiting for the doctor or the dentist with the brain going into overdrive.

Saturday morning followed an unfairly sleepless night, as she turned over in her mind the issue; not because of any misgivings on her part of misdemeanour, but rather the concern about what was underlying the allegation.

Sunday afternoon came and with it the email summoning her to the interview. Excellent - a disrupted evening with the psychological sword of Damocles hanging over. She remembered her army brother telling her of PSYOPS as an instrument of war: it did not matter how innocent you were, the aim was to make you sweat in suspicion and non-existent guilt.

Monday came following a mind-churningly disturbed night. The tactics had worked, the innocent made to feel concern through sheer uncertainty, like a hooded mock execution. She dug deep as she drove to work, and deeper still as she went into the buildings. The HR lady appeared almost to have been lying in ambush for her, and sporting a corporate, business-like smile went up to Louise and said:

"Good morning, Louise. The Acting Headmaster would like to see you at nine o'clock immediately after Assembly in his office."

"But I have an A level class to teach lesson one."

"It doesn't matter. Cover has been arranged"

And so it was that discipline took precedence over teaching. And so it was that Louise waited at the allotted time to meet HMD, who kept her waiting for some thirty minutes, valuable teaching time. Finally he arrived with HR in tow, went into his office and some ten minutes later invited Louise in.

"A complaint has been made that you have been engaged in an inappropriate relationship with a student of the Sixth Form, Louise."

"I have no idea what you are talking about. Who has made the complaint?" asked Louise.

"I can't tell you that."

"Which student am I alleged to have been having an inappropriate relationship with?"

"I can't tell you that either."

"Well, you don't seem able to tell me much, so there doesn't seem to be much to comment on, except to say that this is just rubbish and that I refute the allegation. I am not in a position to defend myself since you won't give me any specific details and it would be better that I were in my A level class teaching than wasting my time here. I shall report this to my union rep."

"We will be looking into the issue and will call you back when we are ready."

"Very well, but it would have been better if you had looked into it further first and given me more information."

She went to her class and stood the cover teacher down so that she could get on with her teaching, in what remained of the lesson.

It was the following week that she was called again. In the meantime, Louise had spent many perplexing moments wondering not only if the sword being held above her would fall, but also who was holding it and more importantly why. Common courtesies were cold at best when she passed HMD in her transits around the campus, though he always smiled superciliously from on high.

"Louise, we have decided not to pursue the matter." He did not even have the manners to invite her to sit down, even as he himself lounged in the chair behind his desk. So she sat herself down uninvited.

"That's it?" she said in disbelief. "You have bandied my good name about, disrupted my teaching and unsettled my life; and then you decide not to pursue the matter. What matter was it?"

"We can't disclose that."

As she stood up to depart she shook her head in frustration and said: "My union is aware of this matter. I have got a class to teach."

Chapter 16

THE end of term finally arrived and with it the Christmas Carol concerts. The choir members had been pushed ruthlessly to the point of harassment to give of their best, and they performed in the school and by invitation at venues beyond. The school assembly on Monday of the final week was graced with a fine choral performance and Friday saw everyone gather in the Chapel for an unsurpassable evening of prayer and song.

"Another brilliant rendition from the choir, and that solo! Amazing! I just wish we staff were not parked along the sides where we cannot see anything. Never mind, everyone is going to the bar and we can have some down time as long as the Suits don't come."

But within ten minutes of getting to the bar, the Suits arrived and showed no sign of leaving in any hurry. Those who had ingratiated themselves continued to do so, whilst others saw nepotism, cronyism and favouritism at work, and gagged on their drinks and hors d'oeuvres.

"Come on, let's go; can't stand this for too long: just look at them". With which a group of the disenchanted ones voted with their feet and set off for the local pub before calling it a wrap and going home for the Christmas recess.

The following day was going to be quiet at the school, for all the teachers and day pupils had broken up for the holidays, and only a few of the boarders and boarding staff remained. Menn was up promptly at half past six to have breakfast and be ready for the transfer to the airport. He was full of eager anticipation, having been away from Hong Kong for some four months, and waited anxiously for the taxi to arrive at half past seven. The driver pulled up at reception, made contact with Menn and put his case in the boot of the car. Menn said goodbye to the House Master who had waited with him, his wife Kate standing beside him holding onto their dog. Menn climbed in without much of a backward glance and willed himself to be belted into his seat aboard the aircraft already.

It was cold, and warnings had been given of black ice, which slowed their progress to the airport; traffic was light at first but built up as they proceeded until the inevitable variable speed restrictions hampered their progress. Menn was not unduly concerned, for they had left more than enough travelling time, but idling on the motorway was a frustration, akin to sitting in a classroom waiting for the lesson that the absent teacher was not going to deliver.

Finally, the taxi arrived at the Departures Drop-off bay, and Menn wheeled his case up the ramp to Check-in. Hordes of passengers filled the hall, and blocked his view of the Departures Board, crossed in front of him and held him back.

"Better to be like planets", he said to himself. "All know where to go and how to get there not crossing each other. Nature does not hurry but still gets all done."

He finally got sight of the Departures Board and tracked down his Cathay Pacific flight to know which desk to go to, and made his way to the relatively short queue. By the time he was handing over his ticket and passport he was already on the flight in his mind, and fast approaching home. Twelve hours and several films later, he found himself disgorged from the aircraft at Hong Kong International Airport and shepherded to the queues at Immigration. Two hours later Menn was home, far removed from the confines of the school in the cold of England, but with the lessons learned still hot in his mind.

"So good to see you; so good to see you," and the sunny warmth of the family filled him with a feeling of wellbeing.

"We are going out for a meal to celebrate your return, so we need to get ready. Good?"

"Very good," said Menn. "I know what I am going to have!"

The family headed to the local restaurant where Menn had done a few shifts to earn a bit of money. The staff looked after Menn, and knew what he would be wanting. They sat down and fired off the order.

They watched as the cook prepared the food and Menn prepared himself for the first real meal in four months as far as he was concerned. The waiter brought the food, and as his dish was put on the table in front of him, Menn savoured the aromas rising from the bowl and ran his hands through the steam. He looked at the pink of the shells of the prawns that lay half submerged in the chicken broth among the clams and the white of the pieces of fish and ginger. He felt his taste buds being seduced: food for the gods, he thought and he picked up his chopsticks to take the first morsels from the mouth-watering Seafood Porridge.

SPRING TERM

JANUARY

"The wise know themselves but do not see themselves"
Lao Tsu
(604 BC – 531 BC)

Chapter 17

Due to difficulties at the last moment, Menn's flight back from Hong Kong was delayed by several hours, and it was a weary and jet-lagged young man who finally arrived back at school. He had missed the first day's lessons, got himself to bed and feeling vaguely better the next day he went off to his first lesson.

"Good morning Upper Sixth, and welcome back after the Christmas break. Santa visit everyone?"

A murmur of confirmation rippled around the room as the eight students waited for the A level Psychology class to start. Amanda Black had introduced Psychology as a subject to this group over a year ago, and although they were well disposed, they found some of the concepts bewildering - teenagers have a tendency to see life in an idealistic way, and the lessons here were challenging. Menn sat in on the lessons in order to develop his vocabulary and listening skills, though today he was struggling with tiredness. Nonetheless, he always found the class fascinating, and got on well with the teacher as she presented the new concepts.

"Ok, so can anyone tell me what plant this is?" Amanda held up a plant in a pot that she had put prominently on the table. No? It's small, very beautiful but delicate, isn't it? No offers? Let me tell you the story."

She went on to explain the mythological story of Narcissus who rejected the advances of the nymph Echo and fell in love with his own image reflected in a pool of water. Being unable to consummate his love, Narcissus lay gazing at himself in the pool hour after hour, and finally changed into a flower. With which she held up the potted plant.

"Let me present to you - Narcissus!" Everyone clapped and made Ahh noises.

"Ok, good people, notebooks out and pens to the ready, because it is important that you get the salient points about this condition. Not only is it interesting, but it's always possible it might come up in the exam!"

Notebooks and laptops landed on the student desks, and the hubbub died down as everyone got ready.

"Firstly, whilst Narcissus was in love with himself, in Psychology the term Narcissism more accurately refers to someone who is in love with an idealised self-image. Deep down inside such people feel like the "ugly duckling", disenfranchised, wounded and inadequate. Why do you think they might feel like that?"

Hands shot up.

"They were not given enough genuine praise when they were little." "They are out of their depth socially or professionally." "They know they are not as good or clever as other people around them."

Amanda was pleased. They had not forgotten everything over the Christmas break.

"Well done - so a whole heap of environmental factors. Maybe they were led to believe they were better than they really were, and the truth is a bitter pill. So they live life like an actor. But bear in mind that equally it may be due to genetic inheritance, the way their brains are wired up.

Now, in a conversation with such persons, what do you think they will be doing? Asking you about you, or telling you about them?"

"Talking about themselves", said Alice from the back of the room.

"Do you think they will be able to empathise with you about your cares and concerns?"

"No", came the chorused reply.

"Alright," said Amanda as she stood in front of the electronic whiteboard. "Here are some of the points to take down," and she revealed them one by one:

- Hypersensitivity to insults or imagined insults, leading to a **narcissistic rage** of uncontrolled anger.
- Detesting those who do not admire them - **narcissistic abuse.**
- Flattery towards those who admire and affirm them - **narcissistic supply.**
- Pretending to be more important than they really are.
- Bragging about their achievements and then exaggerating them.

She left the bullet points on display and as the students made notes she added:

"A very famous yoga guru, Paramhansa Yogananda, said: 'Some people try to be tall by cutting off the heads of others'; eliminating the opposition. We are all guilty of some of these issues at one time or another," she said as they wrote. "But the point is this: how many of them and how frequently? Because the

Narcissist does most of them most of the time."

She was about to continue when the door to the classroom opened, and the now Headmaster, (HM), stepped in with the Assistant Head, (AH). They were doing their rounds dropping in on classes randomly, checking on who knows what. For non-teaching managers it filled their time, and disrupted classes, adding nothing to the learning.

In other class visits the newly-appointed AH had burst in challenging "Who threw that piece of paper?" when there was no evidence of thrown paper and disbelief on the face of the teacher. The disruptive duo stayed some five minutes: HM nodded in ignorance at the delivery of Amanda, nodded in conspiracy at AH, and nodded his way out of the room.

As the door closed, Amanda felt the eyes of the group uncertain where to look.

"What was that all about, Miss?"

"Who knows, but well done everyone. OK, leave everything where it is, good people; let's just pop outside for a moment. Follow me," and she led them out to an expanse of wall that separated the corridor from the outside world.

"Reality check for you, a bit of a philosophical question - what is on the other side of the wall?"

The group knew well enough. It gave onto one of the walkways around the campus. They had spent years walking it as they went from class to class. But they also knew their teacher, so hesitated before answering.

"And if you were the on other side of the wall, what would the answer be to the same question?" They all paused as they thought it through.

"I guess we probably don't know," ventured Martha, a likely Oxbridge student originating from Moldova. "We might think we know: that there is a garden just over to the right, that there is a broken concrete surface to the path …." and she stalled. "But it might have changed in the mean-time ….."

"So what could we do to help our view, our vision?" asked Amanda.

"Put in a window" said someone.

"Yes," said Amanda. "Put in a window and see beyond." She paused for effect, before continuing. "But narcissists put up a mirror and see only themselves. And if you remember your physics, the image that they see is as far beyond the mirror surface as the object is in front of it: in effect they see themselves on the other side of the wall whilst still being on this side."

They went back into the classroom. It was nearly break-time, and the students started to pack away their things, waiting for the word from Amanda. She opened the door and let them go, looking up as they went at the paleness of the moon in the daytime sky.

Menn made his way out, wondering if he would find the concrete path repaired, and whether the corridor he was leaving would transform itself once he had left it.

Chapter 18

BEING break-time, Menn headed off for the Prefect's Meeting in HM's office. He joined the others congregated around the office door, more of an ante-room with its oak panelling than a school room, the advantage of occupying a former mansion, like many another private school. When they were invited in, Menn headed for a chair by the window and having sat down he took out his notebook and plugged his charger into the wall socket.

He assiduously took down the notes that HM was issuing as he settled into his new role as Headmaster and assumed his mantle of command. The need to tolerate no misbehaviour around the campus, and the necessity of feeding back about any discontent; the requirement to give a continual impression of calm and order, a veneer of karma, the smoke and mirrors of management.

"Anyone got anything to add?" said HM as he sought to finish.

"Sir, Sir! Have you seen pictures from Chang'e 4 on other side of moon? Great Chinese achievement."

"Ah, Menn! I have seen pictures from the dark side of

the moon on television. Very good!"

"No, Sir, not dark side, plenty light on other side."

The meeting finished, and Menn pulled the recharging lead from the charger, but left the charger unit plugged into the socket. He stowed away his notebook and lead, tidied the chair against the wall and departed.

His mind went back to December, a week into his holiday back in Hong Kong. He had caught the MTR train and was in an electronics shop in Sham Shui Po down in Kowloon side.

"I need a listening device", he said to the man behind the counter. "Like in spy films."

The sales assistant said that he had a good one he could recommend: "It looks and acts as a USB charging point for mobile phones, just put in a SIM card and plug in to the mains. It will call you when it detects sound and works 24/7."

"That sounds excellent. How much for that?"

"500 dollars. Where do you want it for? Here in Hong Kong, Europe, States, UK?"

"England."

So it was that Menn took possession of a square pin UK version which he paid for and envisaged its use as he held it in his hand. He would be able to listen carefully, just as his Housemaster had told him.

Chapter 19

THE move started in the Geography Department, when a green crusader took issue with the number of plastic mugs being used in the staff room and in the dining room. In the dining room, there was a drinks dispenser on arrival, and another on departure through a sort of one way system. The net result was that the plastic mug first used was discarded when the used plate and cutlery were taken to the hatch, and a new mug taken to have a final drink on departure.

"The mugs need to be discarded separately", the Departmental Head pointed out in a school assembly, "so that they can be recycled efficiently - they are then processed and used to make t-shirts, plastic chairs and other things as well."

It made so much sense and a dedicated bin was installed at the hatch to collect all the plastic mugs, and the youngsters happily took part, wondering how long it might be before they were wearing a recycled plastic mug from the dining room.

It was not clear where the plastic mugs were going after they entered the bin. However, it made a great lead article for the school's bi-termly newsletter. A big headline RECYCLING FOR MUGS, an interview with HM and a photograph of him putting his very own plastic mug into the bin, with a cheery smile on his face, doubtless as he thought of the very positive publicity.

Back in the classrooms, there were two rubbish bins: one for the recycling material and another for the general rubbish, and let there be no illusions as to how much rubbish is created in a day in a school classroom.

"Are you chewing gum, Adam? Well come over to the bin and put the gum in it. And as a general comment to everyone, all the sweetie wrappers, cellophane, kitchen foil wrapped around your elevensies, not on the floor please, but in this bin.

"And normal paper, you know all the scrap, and the important letter you were given to take home, in this other bin for recycling."

They were good kids, and would not have screwed up a letter to take home, and they knew it was a joke. Most letters home were in any case sent by email, so communications with Mum and Dad were reasonably uncompromised. But they were seriously good at putting paper in the paper recycling bin. Old exercise books, rough drafts, whatever was not needed any further, and was of paper material, went into the bin. By the end of the day the bin was full.

It came about that Karl Heffner, a teacher most dedicated to the cause, needing to get some work prepared before the next day dawned, had taken to staying on in his classroom, where he had all the resources he needed with none of the distractions were he to have driven home, settled in front of the TV and possibly drunk a beer as well.

The suite of classrooms all had many original features, as Estate Agent's particulars love to laud. In this case, the single pane windows hinged in the middle and closed irregularly; which mattered little since the cold air of winter slipped easily between frame and upright, and the wood of the frame had a spongy texture to it.

In the quietude after all the youngsters had gone home, broken only momentarily as the cleaner came round with a vacuum cleaner, wiped clean the board, and emptied the bins, Karl prepared the materials that he needed in situ, and left them safely there. It was not unknown for such carefully-prepared work stored to the campus computer to be conspicuous by its absence when called upon in moment of need, or indeed not to be accessible when teaching in a different classroom.

Karl did not pay much attention to the cleaning activities going on around him, but he did greet the cleaner, a twenty-year old from Eastern Europe somewhere, and on her departure he always said thank you to her, in the meantime getting on with his work whilst she got on with hers in an admirable parallelism that smacked of concurrent activity.

It was after several evenings of this routine, that he stopped what he was doing, and engaged her in conversation. He asked her where she was from, and she replied "Poland". He asked about her family and what her longer-term plans were.

"I want to go back to Poland and train to be a teacher, but it is expensive, so I must work hard now to save money for this."

As she talked, she went about her jobs, and because he was paying attention, Karl saw as she took the bin with the paper in it and emptied it into a large plastic bag. Then she picked up the other bin with other general waste, and tipped it into the same large plastic bag.

"Why are you putting both bins in the same rubbish sack?" he asked. "Don't you recycle the paper separately?"

"Oh no, Mr Ruddles he say that he not want to do all that, and just put all in the same bag."

So much for the green credentials, he thought to himself as she moved on to the next room.

Chapter 20

IT was after many requests to have the windows replaced with the sort of double glazed units that had been installed in other classrooms elsewhere several months ago that led to the final straw, hidden in a flower border.

Outside in the walk way, a worker was busily fastening lights behind a flower bed, that at night-time when turned on cast a most delightful green hue as a backdrop, such as can be seen in zoos and safari parks that run a night-time visit programme. Teddy bear flew accurately, and rightly-so, into a corner, and questions were asked of Ruddles, the Estates Manager, with great indignation:

"How can it be that lights can be put up which serve no real purpose other than as a bit of window dressing, when we have requested over and over again replacement windows?"

"Ah", said Ruddles, smugly "we already had the lights so they haven't cost anything."

"And the electrician just happened to give his time for free, then?"

"Well," Ruddles wriggled a bit, before saying: "Well, he

was already in to do a job."

"Well, maybe you might like to get the window installers who were already in on a job just to pop along and do a job in our classrooms." With which final shot the conversation closed, unlike the windows.

Menn disliked the times that he had to attend lessons in these rooms: winters in Hong Kong were damp and temperatures low, but not like the winter that wrapped itself around the school. It was like a cold, wet blanket that finally gave way to the chill of frosts and snow. Finally the aged boiler broke down, and temperatures fell to such an extent that cold air was exported from inside to outside, through the cracks around the windows. Ruddles, however, was noticeably unbothered by the situation, confident no doubt that with repairs to the boiler, all would be well.

His ruddy complexion became ruddier still, as if he were holidaying in the Caribbean, whilst occupants of classrooms took on aspects of cryogenic internees. Fan heaters were supplied that warmed the immediate area around the plug and length of lead. But Ruddles's office was radiating, and Ruddles himself had to take off his jacket, so warm was he as he sat at his desk.

Finally, the boiler responded to open heart surgery, and some degree of equality was resumed as all were able to share in the common warmth. Most were over the moon about the improvement, for others it meant no personal difference.

Chapter 21

ALTHOUGH not mandatory in an independent school, Inset Days were seen as a positive requirement in the minds of the leaders, and without doubt there was value to be derived. Not all parents appreciated the disruption to their working lives when off-spring was at home randomly, and not all teachers appreciated having on occasions to return early from holidays or other commitments to attend the mandatory ritual.

So it was that Inset Training for the staff shifted to a Friday after the school day had finished: beneficial for parents but an extension to a long day at the end of a long week for staff. And the school diary showed that the coming Friday was the designated evening.

"Do you remember the last one? You know, the Six Thinking Hats, when we all had to put different coloured hats on to identify which thinking mode to adopt."

"I remember that," said someone else. "I thought it was a bit of fun, and could see some value in it, but not of a lot of use most of the time in the classroom in teaching."

"Well, it is a problem solving tool rather than a

teaching tool – De Bono devised it and it was bouncing around some thirteen years ago. I must say that I felt a bit like a Dr Seuss character with one hat on and then another."

So they made their way to the common room and partook of the generous light tea laid on: bowls of crisps and Twiglets, a few sandwiches and biscuits, and cups of tea. Suitably armed they sought out a seat and made themselves comfortable. Not that linked chairs are designed for comfort, but that was what was available, and so everyone rubbed along with the neighbour.

One of the Deputies introduced the guest speaker - maybe more of a presenter or facilitator than a speaker, to be fair - and highlighted his educational psychologist background.

"Good evening everyone, and thank you for the introduction: I am Graham Johnson, and I am indeed an Ed Psych: I studied Psychology at Bristol and went on to do my PhD in Birmingham. Largely my work involves diagnostic testing and follow-up. Anyway, I know you are a captive audience, and I know you put some different coloured hats on in the last session you did last term – sadly I can't promise you any such fun, so at six thirty on a Friday I plan to make you think, and ideally give you something to take home with you. Not, I hasten to add, a Chicken Korma, but a tasty morsel nonetheless.

"Let me start off by asking you to help me out a bit as I try to get a feel for the composition of your group."

Graham had that look about him of a practitioner, one who knew what the problem was even before hearing the detail, but happy to change his mind if new information was presented that painted a different picture to the one he had formed. But more often than not, he was accurate in his assessment, the result of years of hearing other stories that had shaped his acuity.

"Can I ask you please to put your hands up if you teach Mathematics." Hands went up in a gaggle in one corner of the room, where the department sat together.

"Thank you; and now could I ask those who teach Sciences to put their hands up."

The HM stood at the back of the room, near the refreshments, and took a keener interest in the crisps than in the presentation, though he did look along the serried ranks as if checking who was there, or not paying attention. At the front, Graham went through a couple more subjects, and noticing that the HM had not put his hand up at any time, he said:

"And yourself, Sir?" The HM had to pause before answering because he had a mouthful of food. He swallowed and said:

"I don't teach a subject". He felt uneasy at having been the focus of unwanted attention.

"Sorry, I chose a bad moment there. My apologies. OK everyone, now here is the issue."

He rummaged around in his briefcase and pulled out a Mathematics textbook and a Geography textbook, which he propped up on the table. He pointed at the two books and continued:

"I suspect that there is probably nothing that any of you can teach these two subjects. Because you ought not to be teaching a subject – you are actually all teaching children, youngsters, young men and women. And whilst I understand the psychology of teaching students, I know nothing of the psychology of teaching a subject, since the subject already knows itself."

It was at that moment that a Twiglet caught the back of HM's throat and he choked. He struggled to breathe, and his face turned red as he wheezed. Head of Outdoor Pursuits was nearest, and he leapt up:

"Can you cough?" A shaking head answered him. So he swung the HM round and hit him firmly and heavily on the back, between his shoulder blades, and then again, and then again, whereupon the HM coughed and cleared the obstruction. He reached out for one of the plastic mugs full of water, and gave it to

HM, who gratefully gulped it down.

HM made his exit from the room and the staff settled down as Graham picked up the threads of his presentation:

"I want to give you food for thought about the learning process rather than teaching process: almost a bit of heresy, since you as teachers are judged by your teaching, lesson structure and so on, and there is a given that if you follow the processes, they will learn.

So I am going to turn the spotlight away from you for a moment, and make a proposal for your consideration, which I call Green Fingers. In the same way that the map of the London Underground does not aim to describe the geographical location of stations, but seeks rather to make the system diagrammatically accessible, so I offer you a framework of the learning process."

He painted a picture of planting seeds from seed packets in a logical way into the seeding tray compartments; some of the seeds would not germinate and would need replacing; all would need to be cared for, checked and watered. All would need transplanting into beds, in such a way that vegetables might sensibly be accessed later – knowing where to find the carrots when needed, or beans when wanted. But some will be beset by distraction: such as bad seed, thieving birds and hungry grubs; neglect in watering and weeding and generally not reviewing the progress of the plant may lead to its failure; not all the plants will be the same, and nor will they necessarily produce the same quantity or quality of fruit or vegetable.

"And so it is with learning and memory: you as teachers, purveyors of knowledge and information, put seeds into short-term memory where it lives for but seconds if not tended. If forgotten, the seeds need re-sowing; if remembered, the seeds need more attention, till the seedlings are ready for transplanting into long-term memory, that is to say into the vegetable beds, where they will require still more regular review, and opportunity to fruit. But not all of your charges will remember the information the same, any more than the plants will all be the same; and what they do with the information, even if they remember that they have the information, is as equally unpredictable as the crop of vegetables produced. Not all of the produce is going to make it to market, far less win the Horticultural Show prize!"

Graham stopped to let the message get across. The staff listened with interest yet looked forward to getting away too, hungry now with the prolonged mention of food stuffs.

"I bid you all a very good night, and thank you for your attention." Everyone clapped, and they got up glad to depart after a long day, and Patsy said:

"Makes sense to me. I like the analogy. So I need to get gardening gloves out, find a trowel and fork, and get to work. Meanwhile, I'm off to the take-away."

FEBRUARY

*"When the royal courts are very tidy but the fields are very weedy
and the granaries are very empty, to wear colourful clothing and
carry sharp swords, to eat to satiety and possess excess wealth is
called the arrogance of thieves.
The arrogance of thieves is no guide! "*

Lao Tsu

(604 BC – 531 BC)

Chapter 22

TUESDAY 5th of February was the Chinese New Year, and on the following Sunday were the London celebrations, the largest outside Asia. So the Boarding House Master and his wife Kate had made prior arrangements with the school hierarchy to take all the Chinese students to London to celebrate on the Sunday. He invoked the assistance of Louise from Drama and he drove the minibus to the station to catch the ten o'clock fast train up; the journey bubbled with excited voices, mainly in one or another dialect of Chinese, eagerly anticipating seeing the spectacle for the first time outside of China.

The Year of the Pig was about to start, most

unlucky for anyone actually born in the year of the Pig, which in the event did not apply to any of the Chinese students, nor the House Master either. Rather ironically it was established by consulting the internet that HM had been born in the year of the Pig, and when the Chinese students learned of this they giggled in the way they do when they are amused or embarrassed.

They made their way to Trafalgar Square, to the Dragon and Lion dances, and music shows; there was an enthrallment in the air: the colourful banners waved ahead of the leaping red dragons that brightened up the overcast sky. The pavements were scattered with food stalls, and the smell of garlic and ginger filled the air to tempt their appetites

"Miss, I buy you good Chinese food; Sir as well. Wait there, I come back with food."

With which Menn went over to a stall, and joined a short queue before being able to place his order. He had seen the sign above the stall, *Kowloon Hotpot*, and heard the two staff behind the counter speaking to each other in Cantonese, so he placed his order for three Char Siu barbecued pork with Chao Fan fried rice, and rejoiced in speaking his own language on the street again.

"Oh, Menn - thank you. Dojeh!" said Louise who had thought to learn at least one word of Cantonese.

"Kung Hei Fat Choi," said Menn. "Happy New Year!"

Menn asked if he could go to Shaftesbury Avenue because there were performances of Kung Fu and Tai Chi Chuan martial arts, so Louise suggested they went together to see it, and to meet up with the others in China Town later. The pair of them set off on the five-minute walk and on arriving at Shaftesbury Avenue quickly found the cultural zone.

For Menn, it was an opportunity to watch and learn, and Louise saw how he flowed, tensed his arms and slid his feet in synchrony with the movement of the participants he observed.

"Ohh!" he said. "Such good moves, control and focus!"

Louise smiled and felt herself lifted by his enthusiasm. The demonstration came to an end, and the participants put their hands together in front of themselves and bowed. Almost immediately two more came out onto the stage. They paid respects to each other and to the spectators before starting: in joint movements they leapt high in the air, turning to one side upon an invisible axis and as they landed sliding to their knees, one leg outstretched: a small target for any retaliation in case of attack. Their hands were thrust forward like the head of a striking snake, and just as quickly withdrawn, as the couple swung onto another line of attack with jabbing feet.

Louise was mesmerised by the agility and speed of what had become some sort of pugilistic dance. Out of the corner of her eye she caught a glimpse of Menn creating space around himself, and being drawn into the moves he knew so well, his whole leg striking out even as the performers did so on stage, his body twisting and his arms thrusting the open daggers of his hands into the air to his front.

"Miss; thank you. So good, these guys. Better don't want argue with them."

"I agree, Menn. Do you want to join the others now in China Town?"

"Yes, Miss. Thank you."

So the pair of them walked off on the short walk along the rest of Shaftesbury Avenue to Gerrard Street. It was bustling with people, jostling around the Pagoda entrance to China town with its lines of restaurants, all with well-mannered queues waiting to get in to celebrate the New Year.

Meeting up with the others was only achieved with several phone calls and trying to stand as tall as possible to catch sight of each other. But once reunited, they all stayed together as a group, carried away en-masse in the spectacle of the Chinese celebration of the start of the Year of the Pig.

By eight o'clock they were once again on the train home, if the boarding house was indeed home, their conversations reflecting the thoughts and memories of the day.

In the same compartment was a group of youths who got increasingly out of control as the journey progressed: they shouted at each other, bounced up and down on their seats and threw themselves against the back rest that adjoined the seats occupied by Louise and the House Master and his wife Kate, causing them to be rocked around with every assault. They exchanged glances with another set of passengers in facing seats on the other side of the central passageway. The Chinese girls were one set of seats removed from the aggravation, and were busy making little videos of each other.

Suddenly, a voice rang out: "Bloody Chinks. Why can't they speak English in England?"

No sooner were the words uttered than one of them stood up and approaching the group of Chinese students drew a knife.

And no sooner was the knife drawn than Menn was on his feet confronting the assailant. Even as the knife was directed towards Menn, one of the Chinese girls turned her phone towards them and started recording the incident.

"Leave it, Menn. And you: put the knife down," commanded the House Master.

But the knife only went down as the backward part of a forward thrust towards Menn, who moved faster, shifting his weight onto his back foot, turning to his left as he did so and raising his right foot to knee level. He pivoted on his grounded foot and kicked forward, the side of his shoe striking against a knee cap before the knife had got to the bottom of its upwards swing; Menn snapped his foot back again and prepared use his left arm to block the hand holding the weapon; he stepped forward to shift his centre of balance over the front foot, even as his right arm thrust his hand hard into the solar plexus; the breath came out of the assailant in a loud wheeze, causing him to double up, and as his head dropped Menn lifted his knee abruptly into the youth's head, knocking him to the floor. Menn strode forward and stepped hard on the arm that was holding the knife, looking sideways as he did so lest others from the group of youths joined in.

The train guard had come upon the scene from the other end of the carriage and appraising the situation had taken out his mobile phone to request police assistance at the next station. He moved forward into the aftermath of the affray and picked up the knife with a handkerchief.

The group of youths fell silent at the outcome of events, pinned in their seats. The assailant moaned from the floor, where he lay unable to get up.

The group of Chinese students were initially somewhat stunned by the incident but then broke out into rapid fire dialect, while Menn looked impassively at the crumpled figure at his feet.

"Control, focus and discipline," he said quietly. "So sorry."

"Well done, Menn!" said the House Master. "There will be some questions when we get to the next station, I shouldn't wonder."

When the train pulled in some five minutes later at the station, there were four policemen and women on the platform, who quickly went to the carriage, directed by the guard. They pulled the miscreants off the train, and took them down to the waiting squad cars. From Menn, Louise, the House Master and his wife Kate they took statements, and for good measure from other passengers seated in the same area.

"Am in trouble?" asked Menn, and the policeman looked him in the eye before replying:

"I wouldn't think so, young man. It looks like self-defence, and there are plenty of witnesses to that effect. The video footage is important too." He turned to Louise and asked which one had made the video, and asked that she forward the footage to his work phone straight away. She accessed the file on her phone, and sent it to him.

"Thank you, Miss. I'll wish you all a good evening, and we will be in contact as and when necessary."

The group made their way to the minibus, left parked in the station car park, and headed back to the school.

Chapter 23

WAY back in the realms of time, namely some three months ago, a call had gone out to the youngsters to get teams together for a night navigation competition with other schools and youth groups, to be held in February, right on the doorstep. The surrounding area provided a great place to be out in the countryside, map reading around the hills with compass to the fore. No GPS, no mobile phone conversations, just honest to goodness self-reliance and some life skills.

Twenty-eight names suddenly appeared on the sign-up sheet, some expected some rather unlikely, but all up for a challenge. Training started, and groups were often out well into sacred prep time, but learning much about pacings and timings, reading a map and relating the map features to the ground and the ground features to the map.

"OK, people - from here to the marker over there is 100 metres. At a normal walking pace, you must set off and count every other step: that is to say every time your right foot comes back in contact with the ground count: ONE (miss) TWO (miss) THREE (miss) until you get to the end. Remember how many you count to when you reach the marker.

Right, first two off you go. Harry, come back - giant strides is very funny but won't help you!"

They finally all got to the end and made a note in a notebook as to how many double steps each individually took to cover the 100 metres. They then repeated the process, this time with watches, or as proved to be the case, timer on mobile phones, and noted down how long it took to cover the 100 metres.

"Sir, why are we doing this?"

"Good question, Peter. Because if you have got to cover 500 metres between checkpoints in this competition, you know it will take five times as long as it took you just then to cover 100 metres, and will take 5 times as many double paces. And when it is pitch black and you have only got a torch to light your way, you need to know that when you get to the correct timing or number of paces, then you are somewhere near your objective."

"But Google would get me there without the hassle."

"And what will you do when Google fails due to heavy fog, satellite falling out of the sky or your battery running flat? Anyway, the competition rules prohibit the use of mobile phones or other GPS devices. This is the use of basic skills."

They were then issued maps of the area, all

covered in grid lines and symbols. Gone were the days when grid references were covered in Geography classes as part of the syllabus – this was all new to most of them.

The weekly training continued, and the youngsters' skills improved. In January the snow had fallen, but that did not stop the efforts, and groups went out and learned not to walk along the snow-covered edge of the track, lest they fell in the hidden ditch; they learned to step carefully, and watch out for the roundel of dark coloured wet snow that indicated shallow snow and water beneath, better avoided; and they learned not to eat yellow snow. For Menn it was all very novel, because there was no snow in Hong Kong, and he relished every moment that he was out in it, cold though it was.

"Well done, you guys. Remember that your pacings and timings for the 100 metres need to be increased, because the snow is slowing you down, and as time goes on and you get more and more tired, it all becomes an effort, even just counting the paces."

The red faces of the groups, their smiles of achievement made it all worthwhile.

"Sir, sir – there's something lying in the snow over there. Ugh, it looks rather dead. What is it?"

Sure enough, there lay a rabbit, frozen stiff, its eyes bloated. It looked like it must have just rolled over and given up on life.

"Myxomatosis," said Head of Outdoor Pursuits.

"Not you too," said Menn.

"Me?" queried Head of Outdoor Pursuits.

"Sir, no Sir. Not you. This Rabbit not you too."

"I don't understand, Menn."

"Must be Chinese for understand."

Chapter 24

THE following weekend was competition day, or more accurately competition night, and in the same way that finally the week gave way to Saturday so Saturday night would give way to Sunday in the Competition.

"Good morning, Ruddles! I wanted to check that we are all OK for tonight's Night Navigation Competition. I did send an email, but need to confirm that we must have the back gate left unlocked so that safety vehicles can get in and out in case anyone needs bringing off."

Head of Outdoor Pursuits had been running the school's side of the admin for the competition for several years now, whilst Ruddles was relatively new into his post as Estates Manager and had not done one before.

"No, can't leave the gate unlocked. Got to think about the safety of the boarders."

"But Ruddles, we always have the gate left unlocked for the competition so vehicles can do a casevac if necessary."

"No, as I say, got to think about Health and Safety of the boarders."

"But Ruddles, there are no boarders – they all always go home for the weekend apart from the Chinese group, and they are all out this exeat weekend with host families."

It was only the threat of the cancellation of the whole event at the last moment with his name on the bottom of the paper that persuaded Ruddles to co-operate.

Seven groups of four turned up at the advertised time, to pick up their kit, have supper and then proceed to kit checking. The twenty-eight youngsters represented 10% of the senior element of the school, giving up a night's sleep to be out all night for up to eight hours, traipsing around looking for checkpoints! There were three staff members running the school team: Head of Outdoor Pursuits, and two assistants, Jess and Nathan; Menn had forfeited his place in a team so that a late applicant could take part, so he had opted to help the staff members out with the admin.

"Ok, guys! Leave your kit in the corridor and get yourselves off for some scoff. Teams leaders, you need to be back here with your team at seven for kit check."

The teams headed off in great excitement and

anticipation of getting going. A decent meal would set them up, and in their backpacks they had rations to see them through the night. The staff paused to take breath as the youngsters disappeared.

Jess said: "You know that tonight is Burns Night?"

Menn looked quizzically at her and asked if burns was a First Aid matter. Jess laughed politely and explained who Burns was and explained about the celebratory dinner.

"Well," she continued, "all the Senior Management are going, most live on site, and just across the way. And you know that the Head of Senior School is over there as well, and most of the team members are Sixth Formers. So do you think they are going to poke their heads in as they come past to wish good luck to their teams? You know, a bit of leadership and man-management, that sort of thing."

"Who knows, be nice wouldn't it, pop in on their way past, touch base with the kids and us," said Nathan. "Probably wouldn't put much money on it though!"

His money was safe since when all the youngsters had come back at seven to pick up their kit, the four DJ-clad upper echelons of management happened to arrive at the same moment and predictably just walked on by and paid not a jot of heed.

Midnight came, and the teams had been out for four hours already, and Jess and Nathan went for a walk around the Competition Admin areas to see how teams were doing on the computer tracking system. It was early yet, but two of the school's teams were storming it, and collecting valuable points on the command tasks. Great! They were putting all their skills to work, aided by the brightest imaginable moon, only three nights short of a full moon casting shadows and lighting the woods like a searchlight.

So the pair of them went with Menn to the dining room where the Burns Night had taken place, and peered through the windows. Within, still seated after all others had left, were the DJ-clad team of four, swigging the last of the wine, and commencing on whisky. One got up and went over to the kitchen, and came back with a further bottle of wine, which they duly shared, and grunted their drunken pleasure. An hour later they finished drinking as a clock struck one, tacked their way along the path like sailing ships and avoided all contact with the reefs and sandbanks of the Night Competition.

At three in the morning, the school teams started to return, de-kitted, and bedded down for the rest of the night to be collected later in the morning by proud parents. The Upper Sixth team came first and won the trophy for the first time in a decade.

The DJ-clad team didn't really care one way or

another.

Chapter 25

A ROUTINE had established itself for Menn over the last six weeks since the Prefects' Meeting in January when he had left his notebook charger in the wall plug in HM's office. The device was constantly charged since it was plugged in to the mains; it was voice activated, and every time there was conversation in the vicinity of the microphones built into the charger, the electronics rang a designated number namely a pay-as-you-go mobile phone that Menn had bought for the purpose.

He left it on silent mode so that its ringing was not heard, and on not being answered it defaulted to answer phone when activated, as a consequence of which Menn could access the recorded messages later at leisure. The phone itself was secreted in what looked like a book with its spine suitably printed in Chinese characters, but which was actually a receptacle for secreting valuables in its hollow innards, and stood inconspicuously on the bookcase with other genuine books. Every day he accessed the recordings at break-times, lunch-times and prep-times, because the system would get overwhelmed if he did not keep up with monitoring and then deleting the volume of traffic.

Some of the recordings were irrelevant to his perceived needs, and were rapidly dispatched to the trash bin. But some were of evident interest, though he did not necessarily know why nor did he understand them fully.

"Look," said HM's voice: "We tried at the end of last term to put her under pressure. I think she was a bit more resistant than we gave her credit for. How much did you say she costs?"

"Forty thousand."

"She's expensive, so I don't care how we do it, I want her gone. I want to release that money. She keeps on applying for jobs but not getting them so we need to pick away at her competency."

"You know, we can afford to pay her off: what we pay in a lump sum will be off-set by longer-term savings."

"Sod's law she would then get a job offer."

"That is the gamble, so if you can't make a case for incompetency you could try offering her, say ten thousand and see how she reacts."

"Uhhm. I think that I'm going to up her work-load, and just make life a bit more difficult, see if we can't unsettle her."

Menn had saved it more out of sheer intuition than strict logic.

MARCH

Chapter 26

A TRIP to the theatre in London had been organised to see Shakespeare's Julius Caesar, set text for the A level English group, and Menn was looking forward to the trip. Probably he might not understand much in detail of the language, nonetheless it was going to be an experience. Somewhat different from the Chinese Theatre he had seen in Hong Kong, very stylised and accompanied by reedy voices singing the story and traditional stringed instruments wafting in support. So tomorrow was not going to come too soon, to have an escape from the rural environment all around to the energy of the capital.

The students taking public exams were feeling the pressure building up, but Menn had no such constraints because he had taken all his exams the previous year in Hong Kong. He had been spared the grief of mock examinations in the first two weeks of term back in January, and his half-term holiday in

February had been genuinely time off, whilst for his peers it had been an opportunity to catch up and consolidate and try to get their minds and memories around everything.

The weather was not conducive to much outside activity: it had rained for ever, or so it seemed. Menn had not been able to get outside to practise his Tai Chi early in the morning before the others got up and had taken to creating space in the Common Room by moving chairs and tables. He would then slip effortlessly into balance and move smoothly and slowly from one posture to the next, focussing inwardly on each transition. The complementary forces of Yin and Yang created a unitised dynamic duality, a whole that was greater than the parts: no old without young, no rich without poor, no good without bad. An inner calm and clarity filled his being, and gave him insight, direction.

Then he would put back the furniture, and return to his room, still before others were up, and spend some thirty minutes going over the new expressions and vocabulary he had jotted down in his notebook. The calmness he brought with him from the Tai Chi relaxed his mind and allowed the pathways around and within his memory to light up and grant interconnected access to the stores of information. His lips silently mouthed the words and the phrases as he sampled, recalled and read the structures, pushing and pulling the vehicles of language into short-term and long-term parking slots. And all the while, his subconscious was processing all his observations.

"Morning Menn," said the Housemaster. "After breakfast, don't forget there is Assembly in the Hall at twenty to nine."

"Yes, Sir," said Menn.

"Do you know what day today is, Menn?"

"Today Friday."

"And what date?"

"Today ….." Menn took out his phone and looked at the screen. "Today fifteen March.

"And do you know what that is, Menn?"

"Yes, Sir. That makes fifteen days rain, it rain all month - too wet. This like monsoon in Hong Kong. Sometimes in Hong Kong we have typhoon and then is very dangerous, with big winds. Sometime water in sea mix with dirty water from fish farms and other crap and so sometime we get Red Tide. Red Tide not red, more like Brown Tide, and we cannot swim and cannot eat seafood. Seafood become very bad and make you sick, so cannot eat. No good. My father, he use work in Department Fisheries, and he text me that

Marine Police found Red Tide last Saturday, so I learn lot from him of this problem. Red Tide! No good."

"It's a case of Beware the Red Tides of March, Menn," the Housemaster said, playing with his Shakespeare. "Julius Caesar was assassinated on this day two thousand and sixty two years ago. Cassius persuaded Brutus to kill him. Don't forget to come to the meeting for the trip during tea-break this afternoon at half past four in the Meeting Room and learn some more. Anyway, Menn – off you go to breakfast, and I'll see you in Assembly."

Menn headed off for breakfast in the dining room, wondering who Cassius and Brutus were, but expecting to find out later. He headed back from the dining room and on to his duties. As a prefect, Menn stood at the door to the Assembly Hall and quietened down the youngsters as they came in, and helped the teachers send them to their seats. This was never an easy task since many of the pupils were boisterous, necessitating attention to effect as rapid an entry as possible.

While everyone assembled, Menn watched as HM joshed about with his deputies, as if in another context altogether. He stood deep in interrogation with his mobile phone, eyes fixed on the screen; and then he turned to his right-hand-man and made a jocular remark that right-hand-man dutifully laughed mirthlessly at; the pair of them rocked and swayed with a swagger that suggested ownership of the universe and contempt for all that was not of their machination. Finally everyone was quiet and HM started his address. He liked to run the show and kept himself centre of attention like some celebrity on stage entertaining the paying public, or perhaps still rehearsing in front of a mirror and seeing himself reflected.

Suddenly, one of the panels that formed a false ceiling above the assembled group bent in the middle. It had softened with the rain water that had seeped in through the roof panels and finally a critical mass was reached whereby the downward force was greater than the resistance, until finally it slipped from its stays and fell.

Nobody saw it happen, only the aftermath, as it crashed down onto Menn, sitting directly below. It landed on his knees, narrowly missing his head, and broke into sodden pieces of fibre on the floor. He leapt up, and looked above him at the gaping hole in the ceiling, brushed himself off and walked out of the Assembly Hall. His Housemaster who was sitting a bit further down the row of staff seats got up out of his seat and followed him out. The pair of them stood under cover outside as Menn regained his composure, surprised that the remainder of the Assembly did not follow suit; but HM was carrying on with his Assembly, wrapped up in his own importance, not giving thought to the simple fact that if one panel had slipped, then others might follow.

Since HM did not seek out Menn, Menn took it upon himself to seek out HM. He went to the office at break-time and asked for an appointment to see HM, who was very busy until lunch-time, but maybe Menn might talk to HM as he stood supervising the lunch queues.

"I no stand in Dining room talking this matter. I need proper interview time. When I can see?" insisted Menn, dust and ceiling panel fibre still clinging to his trousers.

"Well, after lunch at two o'clock, Menn. May I ask what it is about?" said the PA, fingers poised above her keyboard. Menn thought to smile and not listen, but said:

"Private matter, personal please."

The morning slipped by, and at five minutes to two Menn was outside HM's office. Ten minutes later Menn was still outside the office, and was still there five minutes later as well. Finally HM arrived and invited Menn inside.

"Menn, what can I do for you?"

"Sir, I not happy about this morning. Ceiling fall down and land on me – not good. Dangerous."

"Menn, I am so sorry. How are you? Frightening for everyone else around."

"Sir, one piece ceiling fall down, maybe more piece might fall down – not good, and my Civil Defence Training tell me need to empty hall, not carry on. Very dangerous, not good."

"Menn, I will decide if it is too dangerous to continue, not you." HM felt threatened by the comments made at him, the attack on his sovereignty, and adopted a protective stance. "I did a quick evaluation of the risk, and decided the Assembly could and should go on: I had important things to say, and we did not see any imminent danger."

"Sir," said Menn. "Sir …." But he was cut short by the peremptory end to the meeting as HM stood up saying that he was sorry but he had another meeting to be at, and showed Menn to the door.

Menn shook his head as he exited, not understanding why HM could not see the potential danger he had put everyone in by not clearing the Assembly Hall. On returning to his room, he rang his father in Hong Kong, where it was already evening and in rapid Cantonese told him what had happened, the tones creating the sharp, angry, staccato delivery of the message. His father was unimpressed and offended that his son had been involved, and that others had been put at risk. He felt for his son and told him to be patient, for soon he would be home for three weeks holiday for Easter. Then they could talk.

Chapter 27

At a quarter past four, Menn headed off to the Meeting Room for the briefing about the next day's trip to London.

"Ok Guys. You have got the trip to London tomorrow to see Julius Caesar, so I am going to paint you a picture of this character. Sixty years before Christ, Caesar and two others set up a political alliance that was to control the politics of Rome. They were power-hungry and tried to set up a power base representing the ordinary people, and although this was thwarted, Caesar gained credibility and power through his military victories especially in France. He built an amazing bridge over the Rhine, and invaded England. All great achievements, all inflating his self-image, but these were not wars sanctioned by the Senate in Rome, rather the work of a renegade.

He was summoned back and did so only under arms, crossing the Rubicon to engage in civil war. The Senate showed weakness and effectively fled, leading finally to Caesar's success and appointment as dictator. Wars followed wars as Caesar consolidated his position as the greatest military strategist."

"This sound like days of Chinese Kings and Emperors," said Menn. "Much power, much fightings and many rebellions. No teachings, no learnings, much subjugations." He paused for a thought to materialise before continuing: "But Sun Tzu, he say *'A leader leads by example, not by force.'* This Caesar, he no lead by example, much force."

"Thank you, Menn – always a valuable contribution to make, and I appreciate your comment. Just an aside before I finish, the name Caesar lives on in a different form: in Latin it is a hard letter C so it sounds like KAESAR, and the Germans had a Kaiser or Emperor, and the Russians had a Czar, also Emperor. How do you say Emperor in Chinese, Menn?"

"Sir, in Chinese is Huangdi. No connection!"

"True enough, Menn. Well, they have in common that ultimately they were out of touch with the people, and failed. OK, everyone: I will see you at half past four, tomorrow, on the car park; smart but casual please: chinos not jeans etc. You know the drill: you are representing the school, so good behaviour. Any questions? No? OK, off you go, see you all tomorrow."

Tomorrow came, they boarded the coach and set off for London. The coach drove parallel to the Thames, along Tooley Street and dropped the group off to walk through Potters Fields Park to get to the

Bridge Theatre. They took their seats and waited with uncertain anticipation.

"You looking forward to this, Menn?"

"Yes, Sir; this will be excellent. Very powerful. I have read article on internet about play. I think many lessons in theatre today."

The lights dimmed and marked the start of a modern-dress production of Julius Caesar, a character bent on absolute power, resonating in the minds of the audience conscious of a world witnessing a slide into tyranny: the political corruption of morals.

"Sir, can imagine if Caesar not die? Brutus did him favour to kill him, so he not get corrupted with too much more power." Menn delivered his thoughts soberly after the performance. "Already bad enough. Need strong man to get power and not get corrupt. We say: *solve one problem and you keep a hundred away.*"

"And we say 'Power corrupts', Menn. Maybe also it can be that powerful men fear losing power and it is that which corrupts, makes men do bad things." Menn thought about that, and consigned it to the depths of his mind to ponder more.

Chapter 28

MENN had listened on his phone to many conversations, some face to face, others by telephone, transmitted from HM's office, struggling to keep up with the volume of the task. He sat for an hour with his earphones in trying to decipher what was being said and whether it was important. Important for what he would not know until he had heard enough and had a picture forming, but he did know that you cannot have too much information.

"Your job is to keep discipline in the Boarding House, and I'm getting fed up with that Chinese student: Ming."

"We don't have a Ming, would that be Menn?"

"Yes: Menn. He has an oriental arrogance about him, and I didn't appreciate being taken to task over that ceiling panel coming down."

"Well, I suppose that he has a point really: it was a fundamentally dangerous situation."

"And I don't expect you to be taking his side."

"I'm sure you don't, but at least let's be glad he isn't suing for negligence, or damages."

"Rein him in — ever since that incident on the train the others almost hero-worship him. Like he's some sort of ditty. Rein him in, dammit."

"Some sort of ditty, Headmaster? Would that be 'some sort of **deity**' perhaps? I'll talk to him, Headmaster. Leave it to me."

"See that you do. And bring me a progrom of what you intend to do."

"Progrom, Headmaster? Programme, perhaps? Let me talk with him."

Menn sought out the House Master in his office, and wondered how to approach the issue with discretion.

"Sir. Can I talk?"

"Yes, Menn. Of course you can. Come on in. What's the problem?"

"Sir, I think Head no like me."

"Why would you think that, Menn?"

"The way he look at me, not speak, ignore me and like he look through me."

"I'm sure it isn't like that, Menn. Try to avoid challenging him, perhaps …."

"I not challenge. I listen lots. Sir, what is 'deity'?"

"It means god, Menn. Why do you ask?"

"Sir, maybe I god; maybe Head afraid I god, and he not god."

"Menn, I think it is best that you continue to do good things, that you do the things that are necessary. You will be fine. Things are as they are and they are not going to change without a radical and fundamental change, so don't go asking for the moon, 'cos it's not going to happen."

"Sir, you are right. I not ask for moon. Why ask for what already have?" Menn inclined his head in the slightest of bows and went off, planning his plans and plotting his plots.

The House Master was pleased, for he had complied with his obligation. He had spoken with Menn, he had reined him in by focussing his attentions and he had given him directions. He rang his wife to keep her informed of the outcome.

Menn was hungry after so much listening and talking and it was time for lunch. Today he was not on duty at the lunch queue, of which he was glad. Queues for lunch were like queues in Hong Kong, disorderly and with much pushing, needing good control and much patience by prefects and staff.

As a prefect but not on duty, he could go in directly as a privilege, so he made his way past the front of the line, acknowledging as he went an almost reverential set of greetings from the pupils in the queue:

"Hey, Menn." "Hi, bro'!" "Cool, man." He smiled and nodded at them: "Hi guys. You good? Enjoy meal."

When he got inside the building, he saw HM standing at the servery, plate of food in hand, eating on the hoof, being a laudable presence at the servery to hurry pupils through, but forking food to his mouth, dropping splashes onto his tie and showing how not to do. He looked through Menn as if not there.

Chapter 29

LOUISE had occupied several humble teaching abodes in the school, and moved accordingly from one to another at the behest of the system. There was no dedicated theatre hall with stage, but rather a stage at the end of the Assembly Hall, which in turn served for other teaching lessons as well as her own Drama classes.

Rather regretfully, the Hall stood between one building and another, so it also served as a short cut for the lazier folks to transit through when necessary to get from one side to the other. This regardless of the fact that Louise might still be conducting her class.

The doors opened on one of these occurrences, so with her back to the offender she said:

"I'm still teaching my class, would you mind to go round on the proper path, please."

There was a muffled guffaw from the class who were facing the trespasser, so she turned round to see that it was HM himself.

"Sorry, Headmaster: it just gets to be a bit of a distraction that people come through all the time as if it were a public right of way. Someone came through yesterday when the girls were doing aerobics, which was embarrassing for them."

An inane and supercilious smile was the response, followed by an exaggerated gait that surely had come from the John Cleese Ministry of Silly Walks. Louise turned her back with deserved contempt and rolled her eyes.

The proposed solution was to move her from that area to a newly created facility that combined other aspects of Performing Arts. Whilst Louise was promised much, she was given less: there was not a lot of space to seat her students and she was removed from her props cupboard.

"Sorry, class. I know it's cramped, but at least no-one will be walking through any more."

Public exams were not far round the corner, for Easter holidays were looming, and no sooner back from gorging on chocolate rabbits than the students would be headlong into their exam phase.

"Just to confirm, as I indicated a couple of weeks ago and wrote to your parents about, there will be a revision session this Sunday for those who want to come in. Look forward to seeing as many of you as possible, nine o'clock."

On Sunday, Louise got to her room early to prepare for the students arrival, only to find the computer with her work on it was gone.

"Stolen?" she thought. Not likely, for it was one of the older machines. She was perplexed, mystified and finally annoyed by the issue, aware that students would be arriving in some thirty minutes. So she did the only thing possible in the circumstances – she cuffed it, well and professionally. She delivered the revision, enjoyed the company of the eight who had come for the session, and sent them on their way to have the afternoon off.

The following day Louise went back to her work table, wondering if it had been a bad dream, or a figment of her imagination, but no - there it was: gone. She rang the Computer Support technician:

"Hi, good morning! Wonder if you can help me. It's Louise from Drama. The computer on my work desk is missing, as it was yesterday when I came in to do a revision session with some students. Can you cast any light on this?"

"Yup; there was a meeting and it was decided to remove it."

"Well, I don't recall any meeting, and I certainly wasn't at any such meeting. So how am I to access my work at my desk with no computer?"

"Sorry, I just do as I am told."

Louise tackled her line manager who denied any knowledge of the business, so she sent an email to HM asking for clarification and for reinstatement of the machine. Everybody denied any knowledge of the removal, apart from the lackey in computer support, and indeed all denied any knowledge of any meeting.

Chapter 30

MENN had been held up doing his prefect duties, and did not get back to his room very early after the morning break. He checked his phone to see if there was any message from Hong Kong, but disappointingly there was nothing.

Then he went to his other secreted phone, plugged in his earphones and accessed his backlog of recordings. He sifted through, discarding the chaff, considering the wheat.

"What I have in mind is some annoyance. Over the weekend I want you to remove her computer so there is a bit more pressure building up. Drama revision or not, it needs not to be there."

"Very good; what do you want me to say if I am asked, as probably will be the case?"

"Just say there was a meeting; surprised she didn't know about it; must be a mix-up; don't know any more about it."

Menn was unsure about the context but decided that since it seemed to involve Drama and seemed not to be very positive, probably he would save it. He put his phone away, and headed down the corridor. As he was approaching the exit, the House Master called to him from the other end:

"Menn, why aren't you in class?"

"Sir, sorry. I late from duty and wanted to check if family contact me from Hong Kong. Sorry."

"Come on, Menn: I need you above all to set a good example. Do you hear what I'm saying?"

"Sir, I always listening carefully. Thank you, Sir. I show how to do things."

He made his way to the Drama room, and through the glass of the door saw Louise at her desk. He knocked and was beckoned in.

"Miss," he said, "Good morning, Miss. We have Drama after school today?"

"Yes, Menn, we do. Are you coming?"

"Yes, Miss, coming. Miss: no computer?"

"No, Menn. It has disappeared like a conjuring trick."

"Smoke and mirrors, Miss!"

APRIL

"He will win who, prepared himself, waits to take the enemy unprepared"
兵法 – 孫子
Art of War - Sun Tzu
(545 BC – 470 BC)

Chapter 31

As March had drawn to its close, so Menn had become more and more excited to go back to Hong Kong for the holiday. However, the chance to go on an Easter camp presented itself, and Menn signed up for the trip to Wales, a country he had not yet visited.

"I need passport?" asked Menn.

"No, Menn. Wales is part of the United Kingdom and you do not need passport or visa!"

The group duly set off in minibuses in the final week of March, driven by those teachers who were prepared to sacrifice their holiday time for the benefit of the youngsters. They were heading for a youth hostel that was to serve as their base for Adventurous Activities for their five-day visit, and darkness was falling as they arrived.

Everyone was tired, and after eating a hastily prepared supper, they all turned in for the night in readiness for a prompt start. But the bubble of anticipation coursed through the veins of the students and they chatted long into the night, before submitting to sleep.

The following day saw them breakfast, pack rucksacks and head off along the Welsh Coastal path. Menn was in awe of the beauty of the rugged scenery and the far reaching seascape, so unlike the view out over the South China Sea. For the remainder of the walking group it was a chance to get away from home for a brief spell, and spend some time with friends – it mattered little whether it was Wales, Cornwall or Brighton.

Tired at the end of the day, the teaching staff nonetheless prepared the evening meal in the hostel kitchen, less Doreen who though well disposed, had opted out for the evening and was sipping her third G&T, getting ever so slightly increasingly under the influence. This was a bit of an issue since she was going to be on duty after the meal, supervising the youngsters getting to bed.

"Menn can do it by himself," she announced with a G&T smile, addressing the remainder of the staff when they all gathered in the sitting area. "He's up to it."

"And he will supervise the girls as well?" asked Jess.

"Well by now everyone is in bed anyway, so it is not a problem," she said, and started on the fourth glass.

"Yes, but who is in bed with whom?"

At that moment, Menn knocked at the door of the sitting area and asked for a member of staff: "Sir, Miss: need someone go to girl dormitory."

Jess got up and ran to the dormitory, and on going inside found one of the girls snuggled up with a lad from another group altogether that was sharing the hostel.

"You, out; now." The boy snuck off rather sheepishly, leaving the teacher with the group of girls. "And you, outside, now." The girl went outside with the teacher, the one with a reddening face, the other with a whitening face.

"Did anything happen?"

"No, Miss. Nothing. We were just having a cuddle."

"Nothing happened? Are you sure?"

"Yes, Miss. Nothing. Sorry."

"Get to bed and we will talk about this in the morning."

The pair of them went back into the dormitory, and the girl got into bed. Jess encompassed the occupants with a sweeping look of disdain:

"This will not be repeated, or we go straight back to school. I am disappointed in this. Don't let it happen again."

Doreen wrapped herself around another drink and thought how lucky that someone had sorted the issue. Menn looked out at the night time sky. There was no moon since it had as yet to rise, and when it did it would be waning, some six days from being a dark moon: the time when dark incidents might happen, so it was well that this incident occurred when it did and no later.

The next day the group was subdued, though their spirits lifted quickly with the activities they travelled to over the ensuing days: climbing in a converted barn, go-kart racing and coasteering. March had given way to April, and it was departure day: pack up and go home. The staff assembled the youngsters on the car park, and with a glum face Jess briefed the group.

"Last night, someone broke into the office and stole the cashbox. So any pocket money that you had left with us has gone, and worse than that the keys to the two mini buses have been taken as well. So we have a big problem that we are trying to resolve, and it does mean that we cannot get away from here any time soon."

"But, Miss: I'm going skiing, and I need to get home." Tears welled in the eyes of the girl making the statement.

"Sorry, but things are as they are."

There was an air of disbelief amongst the youngsters, as they thought of the precious pocket money they had lost, and being stranded in Wales. Menn went up to the teacher who was addressing the group, and quietly said a few words. The teacher in turn faced the group and said:

"Good news, everybody. Thank you, Menn."

She paused for effect, and spoke quietly to Menn, so none could hear. Then she looked back at the assembled group, who waited with baited breath for her words.

"Good news: it's April Fools' Day!" The group looked at her and burst out laughing.

"On the buses, guys! Let's go home!"

Chapter 32

WITH the Easter Camp over, now back at school again, Menn had grabbed the bags he had already left packed and waited for the airport taxi. Whilst he waited he wrote a quick but concise email to the Headmaster, sent it and boarded the taxi to make his way to the airport for his holiday at home with his family in Hong Kong. It was a welcome break from his school life and his responsibilities, but he was not making a complete break: he had set his secreted phone to redirect all calls to his Hong Kong phone number; it was plugged in to a charger unit to keep it working and providing it was left alone and there were no power failures, then he would still be in contact with the transmitted issues.

However, a more pressing issue was the fact that there had been an appreciable amount of effluent dumped in the coastal waters of south China, nitrate-rich run off from agriculture that coincided with warm weather conditions and slow currents in the waters. Since February there had been a number of sightings of Red Tides, as the single cell dinoflagellates feasted on the nutrient-rich banquet and the algal bloom lit up the water with photoluminescence.

The AFCD (Agriculture, Fisheries and Conservation Department) was now issuing hourly bulletins on the news slots to keep the public up to date with the latest sightings. Fish culture zones in Tolo Harbour had already suffered considerable losses as the algal bloom depleted the waters of oxygen and led to the death of the farmed fish stock.

Five years earlier, in 2014, Hong Kong had suffered its worst six months at the hands of Red Tides, and the indication was that it was the result of increased pollution and changes in climatic conditions. With worsening pollution and global warming the constant concern was that a lethal Red Tide could strike any time, though with no means of forecasting it.

Menn watched the television in his sitting room and lamented the deteriorating situation.

"This is now becoming a numbers game. As the number of Red Tides increases, so the likelihood of a toxic strain of algal bloom becomes more likely."

The Professor from the School of Biological Sciences uttered his words with measured concern. His companion interviewee was Dean of Technology and Science, and he nodded in agreement saying:

"Like any other infectious disease, the viruses are always present, just waiting for the right time and conditions. And the protagonist in the process right now is the flow of waste water from the Pearl River."

"Many fish are dying, I have seen on television" said Menn. "And warnings not to eat shellfish or other seafood."

"Yes, Menn. It is in part due to a process that is called eutrophication: an excess of nutrients in the water, and the nature of those nutrients, mainly nitrogen and phosphorous. This leads to hypoxia: the algae can consume all the oxygen in the water so the fish die, and the fish farmers lose their stock. If it is a large bloom, there is competition between marine organisms for the available sunlight and space, so the algae die: in the case of genus *Karenia* for example, they release their neurotoxins as they expire."

"So, why can't we eat clams and scallops and other fish?" asked Menn as he tried to absorb all the information.

"You cannot eat the shellfish because as they filter water for nutrients the toxins are retained in their tissues and they become poisonous; there is also a bio-magnification of the neurotoxic content as it goes higher up the food chain, so when fish like mackerel and puffer become contaminated the neurotoxins in them are present in greater concentration."

Menn was experiencing mixed emotions at the situation: he had looked forward to his favourite congee, but there was no availability of the necessary seafood; equally he was intrigued by the ramifications of the unfolding disaster.

The television interrupted its scheduled broadcast:

"Two restaurant workers were admitted to hospital yesterday suffering from the effects of consuming contaminated shellfish. Their condition is described as critical but stable. Members of the public are advised not to buy or sell fish products for the foreseeable future, and any such produce that is already in your possession and has been freshly acquired in the last two weeks needs to be disposed of. It is critical that the dates on frozen fish food stuffs are checked and appropriate action taken."

Menn's mind was racing furiously. He turned to his brother and said:

"I can go with you on your next visit to fish farms? I will take my camera and I can learn a lot about the problems and can go back to England with something to share." Menn looked earnestly at his brother.

"I will check. I think it will be OK if it is for some sort of research. I will let you know tomorrow."

Chapter 33

LOUISE had survived till the end of term, despite the best efforts of the system to unseat her, but it was taking its toll. She felt demoralised by the treatment she was receiving, rather flummoxed since it seemed to her that she taught well, and term after term put on yet another well-received drama production. She had done well to stand up to a barrage of attack: the extra work loading, the removal of her computer, the general feeling of Big Brother watching, allegations of misconduct; never the less, now that she was away from it for a while, it was in the quiet moments that it impacted, and sleep was to evade her, as was her appetite.

She had been in contact with her Union and had heeded the advice from her Union rep:

"Louise, you need to understand something: in cases like these, it is nothing to do with teaching and pedagogy; it is everything to do with employment law and cost savings by people in power. They have to pursue certain stages to be within the law and will therefore appear to be mentoring when in fact they are gathering evidence to support their position.

Harassment and bullying are unacceptable. Make a record of everything that is said or done; make a copy of everything you receive by email or send by email; do not enter willingly into any Performance Improvement Programme – don't sign or acquiesce since it implies you are agreeing with their case against you on grounds of capability. Teachers in their 50s are disproportionately the subject of capability procedures. Also, give thought to your relationship with your line-manager: might be where some of the issues are."

Louise did not enjoy a very positive relationship with her line-manager, who had not seen fit to hold a meeting with her all year. Indeed, it was an inappropriate appointment since the two ladies were working in similar subjects and the one wanted to extend her empire and power at the expense of the other.

Rather reluctantly, since she was a dedicated professional teacher and not a self-defence expert, she kept a detailed account of her every transaction, the extra work load, the withdrawal of facilities: rather like an accountant who has to justify every payment and record every receipt so that the books may balance.

The *Diary of Adrian Mole* it was not; nor yet was it the *Diary of Anne Frank*; quite simply it was the *Diary of a Victim*.

Chapter 33

MENN had been assiduously checking his Hong Kong phone for recorded messages being bounced in from the sleeper phone left behind in his room in the school. It was easier doing it at home than at school where he had to exercise more care in a more limited access time. Here in Hong Kong he could effectively monitor in real time, although he had to take into account the time difference; he had to listen to much in order to hear a little of identifiable interest.

"I'm still getting frustrated with three issues. Firstly there is Peterson in the Science Department who needs to go as soon as possible. He is a liability; the kids are running rings around him, and the final straw was when he got locked in the cupboard by them. It ends up being a reflection on me at the end of the day, and I won't have it.

Secondly, I'm not sure that I want to be taking any more Chinese students if they are going to be like this Menn character. He had the audacity of sending me a message after we had broken up for the holidays - he had gone on that wretched trip to Wales when a boy got into the girls' dormitory: what were the staff doing, for God's sake? I don't expect to be taken to task yet again by a student, far less Menn. It makes me feel uncomfortable.

Finally there is this Louise female who just never gets to go, and I want her gone, because she is costing me money. I thought that Facebook photo of her doing a high five with that Chinese student might have done the trick - I could have got rid of them both at the same time. I am looking into capability procedures with the lawyers."

Menn reflected on the comments about the high five with Louise, a gesture of celebration and thanks, and no more. He felt shocked that the Headmaster thought it was a way to get rid of Louise and himself. No wrong had been done.

Then he smiled as he remembered the email he had sent to the Headmaster in his best English:

Headmaster, Sir. Many times in my class no teacher. No teacher at girl dormitory when boy get in. No help when ceiling fall down. No good. I tell my father. Faithfully Menn.

Menn felt a swell of indignant resentment at the Headmaster's stated intentions, and his mind raced furiously again. Menn's father sat down with his son and the pair of them discussed the issues that Menn had mentioned in his email to the Headmaster. He was disturbed by the incidents and the reaction to them; he had respect for his son, but was losing respect for HM, whom he had never met but for whom he had held an intuitive and deeply engendered consideration by virtue of his position.

"You must do what you must do in order to see your time out there. Make sure your actions are always honourable" said his father.

"Yes, Father, I will. Always with honour."

The following morning his brother contacted him to say that he had secured permission for Menn to accompany him on the patrol boat that was going to visit fish farms for inspection. He took his camera and put it in a backpack to keep it dry from any spray from the sea.

The launch cast off and headed out to sea for a Cheun Sha Wan fish farm, where the owner, Lee Kin-chung had lost 7,000 fish since New Year. Previously, this mariculture zone had lost 80% of its stock in 1998, due to a red tide caused by the *Karenia digitalia* algae, and there was constant concern. They disembarked, leaving the launch with its bow covered in brown algae, and went to talk with Mr Lee. He was as unhappy with his situation as Menn was with his:

"Why don't we get a single cent, when poultry farmers get HK$30 for each culled chicken?"

"Not good," said Menn as he took photographs of the current stock of dead fish, contaminated clams and empty cages.

"What fish did you lose?" asked Menn.

"Black Fin Snapper, Grouper; shell fish. Too much," said Lee. "Look there, wasted stock," and he pointed to a cage with clams that had been left on the wooden jetty.

Menn's brother went off with Lee to look elsewhere, so Menn took the opportunity to get a close-up shot with his camera of the contaminated clams. He looked around, and seeing himself alone, opened up the cage and took out a clam, placing it on the top of the cage. Then he lay down to get a shot of the shellfish highlighted against the full moon looking down from the afternoon sky.

He slipped the clam into a sealable plastic bag his back pack and moved over to the decomposing Snappers further along the mooring jetty. The smell was unpleasant, but the effort would be worthwhile. He bent down and took two more plastic bags from his back pack. One he used as a glove to pick up a freshly dead carcass; he pulled the bag back over his hand to enclose the dead Snapper inside it, and then inserted it into the second plastic bag which he sealed along its top edge. He dropped the booty into his back pack and waited for his brother to return.

Once back at home by himself, he set up in the kitchen with the two samples of fish. "This should not be too difficult," he thought, "but possibly a bit smelly! It is as well that today the folks are away all day."

He put on a pair of thin washing-up rubber gloves and set to work. With a sharp knife he extracted the viscera and roe from the fish put them into a pan to cook them gently on the hob to drive off the moisture content. While they were cooking he took the clam, opened it up and put it into the pan as well. He kept them moving around a low heat so they did not stick, and waited till they had lost their water, and they had become firm and dried. Finally he took them out of the pan and having put them onto a chopping board, picked up the cleaver and sliced them up into small pieces; in turn the small pieces were slipped into a spice grinder and ended up as fine powder.

Menn washed and dried his gloved hands thoroughly before opening a cardboard packet of Green Tea filled with sachets that in turn held teabags on a piece of thread to dangle in a cup of boiled water. He took out one sachet, carefully opened the envelope and extracted the teabag which he teased open and tipped out the tea. He then scooped the fish powder from the grinder into the teabag mesh, refolded the top and sealed it shut with a spot of glue; finally, he put the teabag into its paper envelope, and with a pencil, marked a faint dot on one corner to identify it. Having eased the sachet back into the cardboard box he put the teabag box in the freezer compartment of the little drinks fridge in his room.

Menn washed his gloved hands again and set about cleaning everything he had used with consummate care; he opened the window to ventilate the kitchen and put all the utensils away, before finally taking the gloves off and throwing them in the bin.

Some 220 tonnes of fish had died from December to February, at a cost of HK$2.57 million to the Hong Kong government. For Menn, 1 gram of fish had dried from 3pm to 4 pm at a cost of HK$0!

Menn was happy.

SUMMER TERM

MAY

*"Let your plans be dark and impenetrable as night;
and when you move: fall like a thunderbolt"*
兵法 – 孫子
Art of War - Sun Tzu
(545 BC – 470 BC)

Chapter 34

Julie from Maths had sent her class off for break, and was intending to get herself to the staffroom for a coffee and the Friday morning briefing. But she did not get there because one of the girls slipped outside on the steps, landing rather heavily and bumping her head on the concrete edge. Julie heard the fall, the shriek and the tears, and scooped the youngster up to console her, deciding to take her to the Medical Room for care.

By the time she had delivered the girl, handed her over to the nurse, disengaged herself from the pleas not to leave her, and visited the staff toilet, break was virtually over, and she had missed the briefing. So it was not until lunchtime that she learned of the key issue coming out of the briefing. She was wont to sit in her classroom with one of her colleagues and eat the salad that she had brought with her from home.

"You missed a lively briefing this morning."

"Uhm, had to take a girl to the Medical Room, and ran out of time. What happened?" said Julie. She took the opportunity to take a measured mouthful of salad and munched contentedly as she listened.

"Well, HM was not happy, because someone had sent in an anonymous computer-printed letter with some observations in it. Goodness me, he went on and on about it, and fundamentally said that he did not deal with anonymous communications, and that if the person who wrote it would be so kind as to make himself or herself known, then the matter could move forward, but without knowing who it was, HM was not going to pay any heed to it. And then, just in case we had missed the point, he said it again."

Julie had finished her mouthful by now, and was setting up the next one as she spoke:

"Have we seen that sort of thing before, like when someone speaks up on an issue and gets shot down in flames by HM! He only wants to know who wrote it in order to get defensive, have a go, and shoot the culprit down!"

"Well, that's it, and it is a sign of weakness. My husband is a police detective sergeant, and he gets frequent tip-offs anonymously about things going down on the street. The team investigate them to check if there is anything of value. They don't want to know who gave the info, they just need the info itself."

"Crazy, isn't it. You would think any information or observations are valuable. I seem to think that not only do we all vote in a secret ballot at election times, but stores and other facilities all have a suggestions box, and it is the idea not the identity that is important."

"Any idea what the issues in the letter were?"

"No, we weren't told. Don't have any idea who wrote it, either. It's kind of funny that *we* have to be transparent, whilst *they* are at best opaque. You remember that teacher, Mandy, who was suddenly and unexpectedly dismissed at February half term? No explanations at all, and when someone asked what we were to say to the kids if they asked, HM got defensive yet again, started to shout the question down, and said to say that it was personal reasons. Turns out, I hear, that it was because she had had a difference of opinion with what's-her-name in that department, who is as thick as thieves with them all. So it was an opportunity to give Mandy the push because her face did not fit. You will remember that Mandy had already upset HM with those rather pertinent comments she made about bullying not being restricted to the playground but endemic in the staffroom."

"I liked Mandy. She didn't suffer fools gladly, so being here must have been a challenge! It's not as if she was a bad teacher – the kids liked her because she got in the classroom and taught *them* rather than just teaching the subject. But she didn't take any nonsense."

"Firm, fair and friendly: maybe those upstairs might learn from it rather than defend against it!"

Chapter 35

MENN had started going to some classes called CACT in January, when he had discovered them by chance while talking to other students in their Common Room - nobody had thought to direct him to the classes as a matter of course and although he had seen them on a timetable he did not understand what they were.

"Menn, you should come to these CACT classes we go to, you might make something of them. We call them CACTUS, because it's easier and anyway they are a bit prickly at times!"

"OK, you tell me what class is it?"

"Current Affairs and Critical Thinking. We look at what is happening in the world and make sure we get a balanced view of the truth. Well, that's the idea, anyway."

"I look when next class and I come."

The next class had been immediately after lunch, and Menn had sat himself towards the back of the room, because he was unsure what to expect. Tom Peters from History slid into the room and smiled at the small group of eleven.

"Good afternoon, everyone. You are all here promptly, and we have got about two minutes before we start; I need to quickly take the register before we start," with which he booted the computer into life and having checked who was present and entered the information, he sent it off. He spotted Menn in the room and said:

"Now, can anyone remind us, for the sake of Menn, what this class is all about?" A flurry of hands went up as the Sixth Formers competed to answer:

"It looks at Current Affairs issues around the world and the need to check the sources of the information to try to establish the truth; to have good reason to believe the statement or argument."

"Yes, Petra: so we can analyse and evaluate. Correct. Well done. As a modern historian, I need to have the breadth of understanding of how the world works, and to apply the litmus paper test of truth. Maybe the Washington Post is telling the truth; maybe Google is giving a bias; just maybe the BBC and the Times are indeed giving out 'fake news'. Can anyone tell me when it was that Mr Trump took office?"

Menn knew because he had been taking his practice exams in Hong Kong at the time:

"Sir, middle of January, 2017. Exact date I not remember. Nobody in Hong Kong believe it happen!"

"Good, Menn. It was the twentieth of January, much to the disbelief of much of America and the rest of the world as well. Now what have been the hallmarks of his presidency?" He paused as hands went up again because it was something that had gripped their attention over the months.

"Reversing most of Obama's policies, firing people, shutting borders, discrediting the press," called out a voice from the side.

"Great. Look, I guess it is possible that amongst everything that he is doing, there has to be something of benefit, and it all depends whose side you are on. So, let us not take sides; let's try to look at events impartially."

He turned the idling smart board on and displayed the first slide: the words CIA filled the screen. He looked quizzically at the class, inviting a response. After a short period of silent thought, someone piped up: "Central Intelligence Agency."

"Correct." He eased the next slide onto the screen, the eagle emblem of the CIA, explaining as he did so:

"The United States of America's overseas intelligence gathering body. Now, anyone tell us anything about John Brennan?"

Petra had family in the States and had taken an interest in the elections because she planned to go to New York to work after her studies. She said immediately: "Mr Brennan had been Director of the CIA up to January 2017 when Mr Trump was elected to office. He was critical of the new President's lack of knowledge of Russia."

"Well done. Very good."

He advanced the slide to show a photo of John Brennan. "Now, former directors of the CIA are given security clearance so that they can give the benefit of their prior experience and continue to advise the White House." With that he changed the slide and showed FBI.

"Federal Bureau of Investigation," offered a voice. "I think they are responsible for domestic federal law enforcement and they are under the Department of Justice."

"That's it - so the scales of justice," and he put the next slide on. "Well, in May 2017 the Director of the FBI, James Comey, was sacked by Trump." The next slide that appearedshowed James Comey. "He had re-opened investigations into Hilary Clinton's email controversy and overseen investigations into alleged Russian interference in and manipulation of the presidential election process."

Menn sat at the back of the class paying attention to the sequence of events and roles played by the personalities. These were issues he was unaware of, and he was intrigued by the play of power. Like Caesar, he thought.

"This left no Director, so the Deputy Director, Andrew McCabe, automatically assumed the role until a new director was appointed." The screen changed to show a smiling McCabe. "But McCabe was accused of making unauthorised releases of information to the media, which he denied. He announced his intention to stand down as Deputy Director FBI in January 2018 and just twenty six hours before his scheduled retirement in March, he was fired."

"Seems like many people fired by boss!" said Menn, noticing a pattern.

"Yes indeed. Well, following McCabe's sacking, John Brennan, formerly Director of CIA you will remember, said to the President in defence of his former colleague:

"When the full extent of your venality, moral turpitude, and political corruption becomes known, you will take your rightful place as a disgraced demagogue in the dustbin of history."

So, as a reprisal, in August President Trump revoked John Brennan's clearances so he no longer had access to the White House, and more importantly, the White House had no access to his expert subject knowledge."

He paused to let the implication of the issue settle into the students' consciousness. "John Brennan fired a shot back":

"My principles are worth far more than my clearances."

Menn put up his hand and said: "In Chinese we say: *'Is easy to find thousand soldiers, but hard to find good general.'*

"Indeed, Menn, hard enough to find a good leader."

The pair of them looked at each other for a moment, before the next slide came up.

"And this is Navy Admiral William H McRaven who said of the withdrawal of Brennan's clearance:

I would consider it an honor if you would revoke my security clearance as well, so I can add my name to the list of men and women who have spoken up against your presidency."

There was a pause. Then the last slide came up with John Brennan's comments to Trump after the president made harsh comments about James Comey:

> "Your kakistocracy is collapsing after its lamentable journey …. We have the opportunity to emerge from the nightmare stronger and more committed to ensuring a better life…."

"What is kakistocracy?" asked Petra.

"Ah, Petra – a very old word that keeps on reappearing when called upon: it means what it sounds like: a system of government run by the worst, least qualified, or most unscrupulous."

"Just need new good general," commented Menn.

"That's all everywhere and everyone needs, Menn. Next time: Aung San Suu Kyi, please check her out on the internet. For those of you who want copies of the slides, they are on the intranet."

Menn went back to his room and thought hard on the issues in America he had heard in the class, and wondered how many more places had the same problems of conflicts of personality; and he pondered where the truth might lie.

He went to his fridge and having opened the box of Green Tea, he took out a tea bag to make a mug of tea. As he sipped the drink, he remembered when he was younger his mother had said to him:

"To tell only half the truth is to give life a new lie."

Menn wondered how many new lies were being told.

Chapter 36

THE dining room was full of hungry students, all sitting at tables of six, eating furiously. A century ago this would have been a ball room for elegantly attired gentlefolk to grace with their presence; half a century later the chandelier was hanging over reluctant scholars sat at highly polished wooden refectory tables that retained an element of the splendour of former days. Now, decades on, there were these smaller metal-legged, formica-topped tables laid out in a cafeteria style that took up more room in an already cramped dining room.

As a consequence, transiting around was difficult, as bodies manoeuvred trays with plates of food and plastic mugs of water towards available seating. The babbling conversations rose and fell in volume as forks fell and rose. Prefects on duty let more into the room as others left, so there was a continual ebb and flow, a waxing and a waning.

Menn sat down with a number of other Chinese students to eat the servings of Western food that they had collected from the buffet servery. They had no sooner started to eat than the fire alarm went off, its continuous ringing bell rising above the chatter in the dining room.

The emergency exit door was at the far end of the room, and slowly it dawned upon the diners that they needed to react to the warning and head in that direction. So a mass of bodies rose reluctantly and moved as one in a disorderly fashion towards the exit, colliding with the chairs that had been pushed back as the seat was vacated. At the door, a spread of youngsters was funnelled into a narrower channel to get through the opening, and outside shins were rubbed where chairs had struck them, and ribs were nursed where elbows had jabbed them.

Menn was not in this initial flood of people, because he had been sat at a table at the furthest point away from the exit door. Being at the back of the movement, he was in a position to see it all clearly. There was no smoke to be seen in the direction of the emergency exit, so it was clearly a safe route. The fire was presumably somewhere in the direction of the kitchens, which were behind the servery, and whilst there were neither flames nor smoke to be seen in that area, it was obviously not the appropriate exit route. So a member of staff stood at the steps in that direction and directed everyone who thought to go that way to the designated way out.

Outside it was drizzling with light summer rain, and inside food had been abandoned and was getting cold, so almost any alternative was better. As Menn shepherded the last of the students out he saw HM, who had been standing at the servery eating his food on the hoof. He was sure he saw HM catch his eye and felt the resentment behind the fixed smile; then, instead of joining the assembled people outside, HM turned and headed into the building in the one direction that could but lead to where the fire might be. Minutes later he re-emerged with an umbrella in his hand.

It turned out, Menn learned, that the fire alarm had been set off whether deliberately or by accident, by someone spraying deodorant near a sensor that had clearly objected to that particular fragrance.

But HM could not have known that.

JUNE

"In the midst of chaos, there is also opportunity"
Sun Tzu
(545 BC – 470 BC)

Chapter 37

UPPER echelons of management were abuzz. Examination inspectors might drop in unannounced to confirm that public exams were being conducted in a correct and proper way, and since they had not paid a visit in May it made it all the more likely that they would in June.

Beyond that, the school inspection team had indicated that there would be an inspection in the second week. Policy documents needed to be signed off by all members of staff, departmental handbooks had to be up to date and handed in for inspection. Teachers were exhorted to be prepared to be imaginative in their lessons to impress the inspector and seek an 'outstanding' rather than a 'satisfactory'.

In preparation for this there had been internal inspections the previous month, with frequent visits by senior managers to classes across the subject range, followed at some point by a debrief on the observations of the 'inspector':

"To be honest, it was not the best lesson I have seen. I couldn't see where it was going."

"Well, with respect, you arrived late to the lesson so you missed the start when I explained to the class where we were going. My expectation of your observation of my class is that you are there on time, early in fact so as not to cause disruption with a late arrival."

"You had not bothered to clean the white board off: it was still completely covered in writing from a previous class. That makes for distraction"

"Indeed! Now, I don't believe that janitorial duties are in my job spec, although I'm sure most of us do more than our fair share of tidying up after the youngsters – those notes on the whiteboard were your notes from your last class, and you, Sir, did not have the good grace nor the good manners to clean up after yourself and rub off the whiteboard after using it. So I am unclear who is inspecting whom here!"

In the week of the real inspection, Head of Outdoor Pursuits had a long-standing trip to an indoor climbing wall, located some forty minutes' drive away. One of the inspectors had indicated that he wished to get a feel for the extra-curricular activities on offer, and a meeting had been scheduled for five o'clock on the day of the trip.

As a consequence, Head of Outdoor Pursuits was assisting his charges rope up, monitoring their activities on the wall to ensure their safety and correct conduct; and consciously watching the clock in order to allow enough time to get the youngsters changed and back in the minibus.

Traffic was heavy on the way back, because not only were parents doing their own school run, but an accident on the dual carriageway had reduced the flow of traffic to a trickle along one lane only.

Nevertheless, it was five minutes to five when he parked the minibus back at the school and sent the youngsters on their way. By five he was in the designated room ready for the meeting. Fifteen minutes later he was still in the room ready for the meeting, and it was a further five minutes before the inspector arrived. He did not apologise for his tardiness, and Head of Outdoor Pursuits looked at him, wondering how he had managed to plan for a twenty-mile journey and arrive on time, but the inspector had not managed to arrive on time with a twenty-metre journey.

The inspector quizzed him about the activity programme that was on offer and as to what the up-take was amongst the students. He wanted to know if there was enough time made available in term-time and whether he felt supported by the school in the provision of the outdoor pursuits. Finally he asked him if he had any general comments.

"Some teachers see no more than their own subject and offer nothing else, working nine to five: so they resent losing youngsters from class sometimes when they go off on an activity, lest it reflect on their exam results. My view is that education should be a well-rounded experience offering as many opportunities as possible, broadband and not narrowband. So I welcome any support that I can get to open up the horizons of these students. Support, generally speaking, is not too bad."

"Good job, well done."

Chapter 38

SPORTS Day absorbed everybody: teaching staff manning the activities, students either earning team points or shouting support for those who were competing. Rivalry was intense amongst the competitors, often friends off the field but adversaries on it.

The weather was kind, and the sun shone from a cloudless blue sky: shade and hydration were issues to allow for, and bottled water was made freely available for all and sundry. Parents had arrived with picnics, rugs and straw hats.

Menn was not perturbed by the hot weather: Hong Kong was hot in the summer, and humid as well on many an occasion. He had taken part in many a Sports Day in his school, but as he made his way to the briefing for all competitors, he cast his mind back to four years ago.

He was on a sports field in the New Territories where his school was holding its track and field events, and the programme was well under way. Menn was recovering at the end of the track after the 200 metres event. He had been standing with his hands on his hips, pulling oxygen in deeply, his head tilted back towards the sky. As he straightened up and brought his head forward, he caught sight of a javelin being launched into the air, but not on the intended trajectory: instead it flew wide of its boundaries heading noiselessly for a group of bystanders.

There was a hush like the lull before a storm and then an explosion of shouting as warnings were voiced, all too belatedly. The missile found a target, and having hit a pupil, penetrated and pierced an exit hole, leaving the child impaled.

Menn remembered the Fire Services attending, cutting the javelin off, and the Paramedics taking the youngster to hospital. He recalled that many weeks later the pupil was back at school, having had the good fortune not to be seriously injured – somehow the weapon had missed all vital organs and slipped between ribs.

The incident was in his mind as he carried out his designated duties on this Sports Day, namely measuring distances in the shot-put stand. He had stood back from the area in the lull between competitors: those that were also involved in a track event would arrive after that event, so there was a moment to stop and relax until they arrived.

Menn stood looking at the phone in his hands, when suddenly he became aware of hearing silence; he was hearing the sound that follows a sharp intake of breath, and holds before re-emerging as a shout. Menn knew that sound; he had heard it before. He looked round to see a discus flying through the air towards him like some god-sent bolt, even as a combined voice shouted the warning to him. He watched the disc, saw its trajectory and calculated when and where to move:

he sidestepped and the discus expended its energy on the grass beside him. He looked at it with contempt.

Elsewhere, Head of Outdoor Pursuits and Louise had been allocated to the sand pit for Long Jump and Triple Jump. One of the students had smoothed the surface with a wooden rake and everything was ready for the next competitor.

As the sand flew with the landing of the next jumper, Louise was buzzing. When the Inspector had come into her class, the youngsters had been treasures, participating with commendable enthusiasm. They nearly always did, but there was always the chance that on the one day of observation they would not perform: it was a given not to work with children or animals.

She had come up with a great idea for a series of lessons that really brought together Drama, Performing Arts and Music, all with an oriental touch. She had combined Holst's The Planets suite with a dramatic interpretation of the music, but then linked it with Chinese astrology, the role of the planets and the life forces of Yin and Yang.

Menn had come in to help with the aspects that related to the Chinese Philosophy:

"Back in February we celebrate Chinese New Year, and now we in Year of Pig. We believe our future, our destiny can be determined by planets and their position when we born: this is Zi Wei Dou Su. Also in China is the Five Elements: we call this Wu Xing. We have Five

Planets, Five Phases, Five Movements and more. This tell us about everything: political party, how body work, what medicine is good, and all things. So we very respectful of system of five. Today you do Mars planet with teacher, and this planet is about Fire, Phoenix bird, Summer."

"Thank you, Menn. Now, what colour is Mars?" Louise asked the class.

"Red," came back a chorus response.

"Is that a calming or an energising colour?"

"Angry colour!"

"Peace or war?"

"War."

Louise gave the youngsters a set of roles to consider and having talked it through, they went on to perform, stimulated by a video of the BBC proms playing Holst's Mars on the screen, the conductress Susanna Malkki drawing the anger and ire out of the musicians. The students were drawn into the drama, responding to the music even as they interacted with each other.

The Inspector scribbled his notes down, but spent more time watching with a smile on his face as he felt the energy and involvement of the youngsters.

"Louise, what a splendid lesson. Well done."

In the debrief to the Headmaster at the end of the week, Menn was to hear:

"We have seen good and outstanding classes, probably the best one being an imaginative lesson from your Drama teacher. The children showed excellent engagement.

We feel that there are many management issues that need addressing, but generally consider the school to be in fairly safe hands."

So it was then that, following her positive performance, Louise was still buzzing as she called out the distances achieved by the jumpers in the Triple Jump. Once the last competitor had finished, Louise waited to be tasked and wondered if she was for the High Jump next.

The results from the events had been collected, collated and correlated to ascertain which House had won, and cups had been presented to worthy Captains and applauded by doting parents.

Chapter 39

LOUISE had gone back to her teacher's desk, and was gathering her papers to leave the surface tidy for the night when a messenger arrived: not quite Mercury the Winged Messenger who would form the basis for her next lesson based on The Planets; rather was it a minion of the upper echelons bearing a white envelope marked Personal and Confidential.

The messenger left and Louise looked at the envelope with sinking heart, as if it were a letter bomb that had landed on her now tidy desk. She moved it from left to right and then back again. It was going to be a difficult move to open it, but she summoned up the strength to peel the envelope open and extract the letter.

The financial inducement to soften the severance was not enough to offset the feeling of nausea that welled up. A dozen years of dedicated effort was to be terminated by hand of an abuse of position in a prolonged power play. She saw a figure appear at the window of the door, and she saw HR hovering like some sort of vulture circling: Louise waved her away, shaking her head as she did so. The co-ordinated attack did not reflect any co-ordinated support given to valuable but not valued staff.

Louise rang her union rep and described the severance to her. Her rep's immediate response was that she knew about the school and its practices and told Louise not to take it as a personal or professional indictment. She indicated that the meeting proposed in the letter for two days' time was unrealistic and unacceptable, and told Louise to have it deferred. It would not be until the following week that she could come down. In the meantime, the matter would be passed to the legal team for advice.

How could a desire to be in the classroom and impart education and experience to the next generation have boiled down to this, she thought to herself.

She looked around the familiar surroundings, and thought of the many Drama productions that she had put on over the years, the fun and fulfilment for both herself and the youngsters. She needed not to doubt her capability as a teacher, but to keep the faith.

The sword of Damocles was no longer held by a thread.

Chapter 40

SPEECH Day was one of the highlights of the school calendar: an opportunity for the academic achievements of students to be rewarded, for the guest speaker to give words of inspiration and for the management to bask in the glory.

For the teaching staff it was the sole time to put on their hard-earned academic regalia and they presented a powerful sight in the colours of the universities they had studied in. They took the front rows, and parents filled the hall in the remaining seats, keen to see the spectacle, especially if their child was a prize-winner.

Recipients of prizes and awards were chosen by a sort of ballot: teachers made their nominations, management ratified or rejected, and students either received or did not receive, as much for academic criteria as for political decisions.

Menn already knew that he was not going to get an award, even though he had been put up for the International Student prize. He was vetoed by the Headmaster. He had listened to the discussions on his phone, so he was neither surprised nor disappointed. Neither was he taken aback by the fact that Louise was going to be leaving, for he had been privy to that as well.

The prizes had been handed over to the prize-winners, the guest speaker had spoken his words of wisdom and the Chairman of the Board of Governors had stood up.

"Well done to all the award-winners, well-earned I am sure; thank you to our guest speaker, and his motivating words for our youngsters. Always at the end of the academic year there are members of staff who move on, and we are always sorry to see them go. We have a dedicated team and they will have given us valuable service.

I would like to say a particular thank you to the Headmaster for his sterling work since he took office."

As the round of applause rippled in the hall, Louise felt her neck bristle, and Menn felt a shaft of power and determination course through his being.

JULY

*"If you wait by the river long enough, the bodies of your
enemies will float by"*
Sun Tzu
(545 BC – 470 BC)

Chapter 41

MENN had opted to stay on until the end of term, and made himself very useful to the kitchen staff. There were always a lot of barbecues and small functions for students, parents and, occasionally, staff in the summer term once the heavy exam period was over, and never enough helpers. Back in Hong Kong Menn had sometimes helped out in the restaurant near where he lived, to earn a few dollars pocket money, and he had learned the art of attending to customers and serving their food efficiently. So he helped out in the dining room when the youngsters were having their lunches, and because he was good at his job, he was always called on to help at the more public events as well, which often conflicted with a need to serve the pupils in the dining room even as serving staff were needed in the marquee down in the grounds.

When he learned of the Asian-themed supper to round off the Academic Year, he immediately offered his services and his expertise, and was invited by the chef to talk through the menu to ensure authenticity. Menn was delighted, and advised him on specific ingredients that ensured the real Hong Kong flavour. He then asked the Catering Manageress:

"Can I please to have the honour of serve the top table? I very good with this Chinese food."

The guests assembled at half past seven, made small talk and drank their wine, or in a few cases beer. The serving staff was assembled at the servery ready to spring into action. At eight o'clock the gong sounded, and HM and his entourage made their way to the top table, set at right angles to the other tables, as if to emphasize importance – no round table philosophy here. The other guests took their seats at the other tables that were orientated towards the top table like lines of magnetic force.

Menn was in his element, for the theme was Asian, and to start with was his absolute favourite: seafood congee, given pride of place as the starter, described on the menus on each table as SEAFOOD PORRIDGE. It appealed to his Chinese blood to have the honour to be serving such a fine dish to the English diners: prawns, squid, clams, fish, pork and ginger, less cooked than assembled into the dish that Menn always chose back in Hong Kong when given the chance. Why did Chinese restaurants in England never use ginger in the dishes they prepared, he wondered; it never tasted good like at home!

He was charged with the singlehanded priority of starting by serving food to the Really Important People seated at the top table, and he hoped that each RIP would appreciate the special dish. As he went to pick up the plates, each with a bowl of Seafood Porridge already ladled into it, he sensed the delicious aroma arising from the food. Will there be any left over for me to try, he thought, as he waved his hands over the rising steam as if in deferential respect. It was as if magic rose from the congee to his hands, and as if magic fell from his hands to the congee: a perfect yin and yang.

He set about his task and armed with three plates loaded with Seafood Porridge he carefully made his way from the servery to the top table. The first dish he placed in front of the first guest, HM himself; the remaining two bowls to the deputies right and left of him. He delighted in the look of wonderment on their faces as they savoured the Shao Hsing Hua Tiau wine aroma rising up from the veritable sea of delectable morsels in the bowls. He hastened back to the servery and went to one side to carefully wash his hands before collecting further servings which he placed on the table for the next guests who far from being exalted RIPs were not even VIPs, mere mortals beside gods. Then he moved to serve at the other tables so as to hasten the process lest the congee get cold.

Menn was in luck, for when all were served their congee soup, the chef called him over to where he had been stirring and serving into bowls and said:

"Hey Menn, do you like to try some quickly? Your sort of food, I think."

Menn rolled his eyes in delight and taking the bowl of Seafood Porridge the chef offered him, spooned the liquor into his mouth, savoured the seafood and remembered the evenings in Hong Kong when he had similar: "Thank you, thank you!" he said to the chef. "This is amazing, just like back home! You put good food in, and ginger too! They all like, no doubt."

And so it seemed: for as he cleared his table, they all said how delicious it had been, and to say well done to the cook. There followed barbecued spare ribs, bought in ready-marinated from the supplier, needing only to be heated through in the ovens, along with the vegetables. A banquet fit for a king or an emperor, and Menn took pride in treating all with such deference that they felt like princes at least.

Chapter 42

THE meal lasted nearly an hour by the time courses had been served, conversations had been held and toasts had been made; the diners were left in peace by the waiting staff, cheese and biscuits, fruit and chocolates duly laid out on their tables. Menn and helpers withdrew which signalled the opportunity for HM to strike his superior knife against a glass and bid silence. Having silenced the minions he stood up and spread a smile around the room, like Jim Carey's Stanley Ipkiss in The Mask.

He felt a slight bit of indigestion as he took a breath to address everyone, and paused to let the moment subside. But saliva started to well in his mouth, and the pains in his stomach intensified. As he felt the muscles of his stomach start to contract, he rushed forward between the tables, half doubled up as the stabbings continued and increased. He got most of the way to the door when he threw up in a passageway between tables.

Menn watched as HM rushed past him heading out of the marquee, and he turned to the cook standing to one side as well and said: "He look sick, he look sick."

"He most definitely is. Not good."

The pair of them looked at each other, and then back again as he was followed by two deputies, who seemed to be chasing after him like bodyguards, but who were also clutching at their stomachs, but who made it out of the room, albeit traipsing in haste through the mess on the floor, slipping and sliding as they went. The three of them found the toilets and retched till they could retch no more, and then retched again.

One of the diners seated at the lower tables was the Paramedic, guest of the Head of Outdoor Pursuits, and he witnessed it all, running out after them, his medical training coming to the fore. He tracked them down to the toilets, as much by following the trail on the floor as by the sounds emerging from the cubicles as he drew nearer. He rushed in, took a quick look and pulled out his mobile phone and dialled 112.

"Ambulance," he said. "Three people vomiting. Looks serious."

The staff had already moved in to clear the tables and bring some semblance of order to the scene. Like the others Menn had been brought back rather urgently and far sooner than expected, but nonetheless they all set to and cleared and stacked the dishes and cutlery that were then loaded into the van to be taken to the main kitchen. That done, they were all stood down and Menn walked back to his room, pleased with his evening's work, and happy to be finished early.

Thirty minutes later a pair of paramedics made their way to the toilets, where the three casualties were sitting, hunched over, with nothing left to evacuate from their bodies.

"Anybody else affected?" asked one of them, and the front of house who had witnessed everything confirmed that no-one else was ill in any way. Everyone in the dining room had now long dispersed, but, indeed, nobody else was stricken down with the symptoms.

The paramedics took blood pressures, and put drips into the arms of the casualties, who were now shaking and shivering with the effects of the trauma. They got the three of them into the back of the ambulance, where they sat them down with bowls. Half an hour later blue lights and sirens announced their arrival at A&E.

The triage nurse who met them was briefed by the paramedics and the casualties were handed over, and taken to a cubicle lest they evacuate more fluids. There the forlorn trio sat for a further ten minutes until a doctor came to see them. He took the detailed account from them as best they could give it, for their stomachs were sore from vomiting and their mouths tasted foul.

HM said that he was starting to feel tingling in his body, like he was wired to a low voltage current;

furthermore, he said that there was a taste of metal in his mouth, almost as if his fillings were disintegrating or he was washing his mouth out with overly iron-rich water; there was a sensation of his teeth feeling like they were loose, aching in their sockets and about to fall out. He looked around him and realised, not for the first time in his life, that he could not see clearly and he said that everything was blurry.

Bloods were taken and sent off for analysis and seeing the debilitated state of their condition the doctor ordered them to be put into Intensive Care for observation; and even as he did so, the other two complained of feeling cold, aching in their mouths, one of them suddenly unable to see anything at all.

"Keep them on drips and call me when the bloods come back."

Their condition slowly deteriorated over the coming hours that elapsed until the National Poisons Information Service indicated clearly that this was a case of PSP, Paralytic Shellfish Poisoning:

"Paralytic Shellfish Toxins usually result from marine dinoflagellates forming Harmful Algal Blooms under certain special conditions, namely so-called Red Tides. These toxins can build up in shellfish like mussels, oysters and clams because they are filter-feeding, and everything passes through their system, which becomes contaminated as a result.

The microbiology team have identified two poisons present: Saxitoxin and Ciguatoxin. Saxitoxin is a Carbamate compound, and Ciguatoxin is a Cyclic Polyether compound. They are very thermostable so that freezing or heating does not affect them. They are neurotoxins and respiratory failure is a likely outcome. There is no prescribed treatment, only palliative care. Fatalities are very possible. These samples show a high level of toxin."

The casualties had developed breathing difficulties, and were put on ventilators, but whilst the other two seemed to stabilise, HM's system was struggling with the assault on his body. The day painfully became a week, and July reached its end, as he battled against the paralysing effects of the toxins, his brain unable to send cogent signals to his organs.

Chapter 43

BACK at school the day after the supper in the marquee, Menn was busy packing the last of his things away in readiness for his departure. Most of what he had bought over the course of his year´s stay had been food that he had consumed, clothes he had worn and discarded, and a mobile phone that sat in his cuttings book. He opened the mobile and checked that there were no recorded messages outstanding before taking out the SIM card, which he put into his pocket. The phone he packed into the backpack that would serve as his cabin luggage.

Finally he picked up his electronic notebook, and headed off to HM´s secretary, who was sitting behind her desk looking very drained by events.

"Miss, so sorry. In last prefects´ meeting I think I leave my charger for my notebook plugged in by window in office. May I get it back please?" He held up his notebook for her to see.

"Yes, of course, Menn, come with me and we will have a look."

So the two of them went into the now abdicated inner chamber, and Menn showed the secretary where he had left it.

"Miss, I sit over there, by window, and leave charger plugged in down there." He went over and pulled out the charger unit from the wall plug.

"That might have been there for months, Menn, because it can't be seen because of the curtain. Good job you remembered, well done. When do you leave to go back to Hong Kong?"

"Miss, I leave tomorrow, so good job I remember to get charger!"

Menn made his way back to his room, and put the charger into his suitcase. He had smelled a bonfire burning rubbish at the back of the Grounds Maintenance area, so he headed over in that direction, and found one of the groundsmen who early in the mornings would come upon Menn practising Tai Chi outside before anyone else was up and about.

"Hi, Pete, Sir," said Menn. "I come to say goodbye, tomorrow I go back to Hong Kong, and I don't come back to school any more." He pulled from his pocket some sweet wrappers, and said: "I can throw these on the fire?"

"Of course you can, Menn. It's been great knowing you. Good luck in the future."

"Thank you, Pete. Great to be here and know you too."

And he threw onto the fire a handful of sweet wrappers, a Green Tea teabag envelope with a pencil dot in the corner and its empty teabag sachet and a SIM card, watching as the flames devoured and destroyed all of it. He took his leave of Pete and headed back to his room to finish packing, and to look for the Housemaster. He knocked on the office door and went in.

"Sir, I leave tomorrow."

"I know, Menn. I know everything," and he smiled at Menn. "Except only, you remember the Lantern Riddle when you first arrived?"

"Yes, Sir. I remember. *Why you go green when you ill?*"

"Well, what's the answer?"

"Because you look sick."

"I don't get it, Menn."

"No, Sir; must be Chinese to understand!"

"Great, Menn. That's really helpful. So, I know there have been more restrictions here than you might have wanted, but have you had to make many sacrifices?"

"Only one or two, Sir. But I need to get back to Hong Kong so I can have some good Seafood Porridge.

How you say it? I could kill for good food!"

The following morning, as Menn waited for the taxi, the House Master's wife Kate stood to one side, playing with the keys in her hand, her dog sitting obediently beside her, as her husband came up and shook hands with him and said:

"Great to have known you, Menn. You have done a good job here. Well done. I will let you know what the news is on HM."

"Thank you, Sir. That will be good."

The taxi drove off, and some twenty hours later Menn got out of a taxi at his family apartment in Hong Kong. A week later he received an envelope from the UK containing a newspaper cutting:

Menn: my wife Jacinthe Kate gave me this to send to you.

STAFF POISONED AT LOCAL SCHOOL
HM DIES AFTER EATING SEAFOOD

Following an end-of-term dinner at the school, three members of staff, one of whom was the Headmaster, fell ill as a result of food-poisoning, believed to have been caused by eating contaminated shellfish. The victims were immediately hospitalised, but the Head died a week later. The other two members of staff are understood to be making a slow recovery. Investigations into the actual source of the contamination are on-going.

It was towards the end of August that a second envelope arrived, a final comment on the incident that had somehow marked the final days of Menn's stay in the UK. The envelope bore the name Jacinthe-Kate on the back where it showed sender's name and address. Menn opened the envelope and pulled out the newspaper cutting, which had a handwritten message spread neatly across the top of it:

I know you will want to read this.
Good luck. Very look sick indeed!

ACCIDENTAL DEATH VERDICT

A coroner's inquest has concluded that the victim died as a result of accidental poisoning, caused by eating contaminated seafood delivered in good faith by a local supplier. He died of respiratory failure brought about by paralytic toxins, believed to derive from shellfish exposed to toxic blooms in the seas of harvesting. An enquiry is ongoing to establish the links in the food chain.

Menn read the newspaper cutting that had been sent to him, and thought that he understood, as much from reading the headline as the content. He thought back to the lead-up to the fateful dinner, which happened to be Menn's nineteenth birthday. In those same nineteen years, give or take a few days, between Menn's arrival into the world and this point in time, the moon had completed its long cycle and was once again back at the same point in the sky at the same phase of its cycle; and it happened to be a point in its shorter cycle when the Moon was dark and was not to be seen until it emerged as a New Moon: a time of conflict between the planets that threatened the natural order; a time of rebirth, a time when the serpent sheds its skin. A time to start afresh with new enlightenment.

"It is all good now," said Menn. "Now with wisdom all can be better." And he headed off to the restaurant to have his favourite dish.

Afterword

The moon has a powerful influence on the earth, causing tidal differences on the waters of the seas and oceans. There is a belief that the full moon affects the behaviour of human beings and animals, and not for nothing were afflicted people called lunatics; there was also a belief amongst the ancients that there was conflict between the planets in those three nights between the waning of the Old Moon and the waxing of the New Moon

The Sidereal lunar cycle marks the return of the moon to its same position, and lasts approximately four weeks; the Synodic lunar cycle marks the return of the moon to its same phase (ie full moon to full moon) and lasts approximately four weeks; the Metonic lunar cycle, the period of time it takes the moon to return to its same position and phase, takes some nineteen years, forming the basis for the Greek calendar, Babylonian calendar, Chinese calendar; and regulating the intercalary months of the modern Hebrew calendar.

Moon Gods and Goddesses

The moon has been seen as a god and as a goddess by different societies. *Men* was a god revered in the western parts of Anatolia, the Asia Minor encompassed by the uplands of Turkey, Armenia down to the Mediterranean coast.

Hecate (Hekate)

The Greek goddess *Hecate / Hekate* was a goddess associated with the moon, magic and witchcraft; despite being a protector of warriors, hunters and children, she was not maternal or nurturing: rather she exacted vengeance upon those who might cause harm to those she protected.

The moon is a harsh mistress!

Harassment and bullying of teachers

In their most excellent book, *Crying in Cupboards*, Pat Bricheno and Mary Thornton explore the issue of teachers being bullied. Managerial agendas are often of greater priority than the value of a good teacher and student needs.

What price education?

Seafood Porridge

This is a truly delicious dish, comfort food at its best! It is a congee soup that is thoroughly recommendable to all who enjoy eating seafood and shell fish. An excellent recipe can be found at the following link:

www.kuali.com/recipes/seafood-porridge/

But to whet your appetite, here is your starter before the main course arrives:

SEAFOOD PORRIDGE - 海鮮粥

100g fish fillet, sliced thickly

5 medium prawns, with shells on

1 large squid,

5 mussels or clams

60g lean pork, sliced

5 slices ginger

1 litre fresh chicken stock

2 stalks spring onion, chopped

250g overnight cooked rice

Pinch of salt

Pinch of sugar

Dash of pepper

About the author

NJ Kyte trained as a teacher and spent many hours, mostly happy ones, in the classroom with students of all age groups. Early in his teaching career he decided to broaden his horizons and joined the Army, serving in Germany with 6 Armoured Brigade (whose insignia is the Desert Rat, *Jerboa*), and in Hong Kong with soldiers of the Brigade of Gurkhas, among other overseas postings.

For two of his twelve years of Army service, he was editor of the Garrison Magazine "Jerboa" in Germany; and frequently wrote news articles for this and subsequently for the Brigade of Gurkhas' magazine "Parbate": from these little acorns an oak sapling has grown!

Having now retired he devotes a lot of time to writing, and helping his wife Jackie run an exclusive mountain retreat in the south of Spain; their grown-up children are all successfully forging their way in life, leaving only Hastings the black Labrador at home.

Thank you for reading this story - look out for the next exciting publications! You can contact me through the contact form on www.escolta–alta.com and I would love to hear from you.

Printed in Great Britain
by Amazon